A Hint of Holiday Romance

Collection of Short Stories by

Pamela S Thibodeaux

"I have found the one whom my soul loves."
~ Song of Solomon 3:4 (NASB)

A Hint of Holiday Romance
Collection of Short Stories
by Pamela S Thibodeaux

Publisher/Distributor:
Temperance Publishing; an imprint of
Pamela S. Thibodeaux Enterprises, LLC
PO Box 324, Iowa, LA 70647

ISBN: 979-8-9895650-4-7

Cover Design: Heaven's Touch Designs

Publishing History: *Choices, Cathy's Angel, Lilies for Sandi* and *Winter Madness* were previously published individually **and** in *Love in Season* anthology through Pelican Book Group 2007-2020
All Rights have Reverted to Author

All scripture quotations, unless otherwise indicated, are taken from the Holy Bible, New International Version(R), NIV(R), Copyright 1973, 1978, 1984, 2011 by Biblica, Inc.™ Used by permission of Zondervan. All rights reserved worldwide. www.zondervan.com

Contents

A Hint of Holiday Romance

Collection of Short Stories by

Pamela S Thibodeaux

"I have found the one whom my soul loves."
~ Song of Solomon 3:4 (NASB)

Dedication

For Karla: *family by blood, sisters of the heart, friends forever* ~

You left us too soon.
I love and miss you.
(B/F/C/S/A)

Thank You...

If you've been a friend/fan of my work for long, you may recognize some of these stories from previous publications—either through Pelican Book Group or limited editions offered exclusively to my newsletter audience. Do not worry that you're paying for reprints of stuff you've already bought and/or read!

All have been edited/updated, and some have never been published in any way, shape, or form.

Either way, I pray you are as blessed as I am by your purchase of this book. If you enjoy ***A Hint of Holiday Romance,*** please write a positive review, and post it at online retailers and websites where readers gather and/or your social media platforms (FaceBook, Good Reads, BookBub, Twitter, etc).

If you haven't already, sign up to receive my ***Newsletter*** and get a FREE short story.

Winter Madness

They met on a cold winter morning in a cozy coffee shop. Not just the tinkle of the bell above the door announced his arrival, but also the quickening of her heart, the slow thud of blood through her veins, the sharp curl of need in the pit of her stomach. Even before she saw him, she knew the minute he'd walked in. A dream from her past.

He turned. Their eyes met.

William's eyes widened and his breath caught. There she sat all soft and glowing. A ghost from his past. He hesitated, blew a soft rush of air to cool the steaming brew he'd just purchased. A sigh escaped followed by a resigned shrug. *There's no way out of the meeting now.*

Only a few steps separated them physically, miles emotionally. One hurdle at a time, he thought, and joined her at the table for two beside the window.

She beamed at him. "Good morning."

Every year of distance, every minute of longing was reflected in her voice. As though she'd waited for him all along, just as she promised so long ago. And again, not so long ago. William scowled. "Snow everywhere, slush beneath, what's so good about it?"

Sienna sighed. "There's nothing quite as lovely as fresh snow during the holiday season."

He frowned. "Lovely? Tell me, what do you find so lovely about the cold and dampness that comes along with the snow?"

She smiled and his heart skipped a thud.

"Always reminds me of what the Bible says about our salvation. That the Blood of Jesus cleanses us as pure and as white as snow and offers us a chance for new life."

He arched an eyebrow in interest. "How is it possible that you're still the faithful optimist after everything you've been through?"

She took a moment before she answered, her voice soft, not accusing. "What would you have me do, William, forget everything God has done for me, turn my back on Him and just stop living?"

William shrugged. God knew he'd never be able to live through what she had. Which is why he'd never settled down and married. Fear of the unknown had always been his biggest obstacle. That, and the fact he'd yet to find someone who could understand, or at least tolerate, his idiosyncrasies. He'd heard all the rhetoric about faith and the power of it to make one's life simpler, easier, and more harmonious. However, he'd never met anyone who actually lived out the concept. Just the opposite, in fact. Nearly everyone he knew who professed to have faith, had lives as screwed up as his.

Not sure how to answer her question, he posed one of his own. "So how do you get through something like that? And don't give me the pat answer of 'by faith.' Explain it to me."

Sienna knew people sometimes found it hard to understand the whys and wherefores of her faith despite the challenges she'd faced in her life. Especially the death of her husband and daughter. She took a moment to send up a silent prayer. How could she explain something so personal and so deep as her faith in God?

Oh, she knew all of those pat answers William referred to, but it was obvious from his response he needed something more. Smiling a little, she began… "We all have a measure of faith, but it's our choice as to what we put our faith into. For instance, what assures you that the chair you're sitting in isn't going to break?"

He lifted a shoulder in response.

"That's faith. Faith that the chair is well built and will hold you. But the faith I have is that God is in control of my life and no matter what may come my way, He will see me through. I understand you're asking how someone gets through the death of a spouse and a child. Believe me it's not an easy thing to do. But true faith lives on even when we don't understand. Even when we don't want to. And there was a time when I didn't want to either. I'll never forget that day as long as I live, or the way God showed Himself to me in my darkest hour."

Encouraged by his rapt attention, she mustered up the gumption to continue her tale.

"About a month after I buried Jace and Olivia, I hiked down to the bottom of Peg Leg Falls. The sky was overcast and gloomy, filled with dark, billowy thunderclouds. Mist rose from the falls. The water swirled and raged at my feet. Everything about that day reflected the agony in my soul. I wanted to die, you see, and I knew exactly how to accomplish the feat. As matter of fact, I went there with the sole intention of killing myself."

His gasp of astonishment halted her words.

Sienna reached over and placed her hand on his, pleased when he turned it palm up and threaded his fingers through hers. The strength of his grip encouraged her. She blinked back the sudden influx of tears, swallowed the lump in her throat and spoke. "I even brought my husband's pistol to ensure no other outcome. I stood there at the bottom of the falls, wanting to end all of the pain and misery in my life, but for some reason I just couldn't pull the trigger. All of a sudden, my heart cried out, 'Why God?'

"I screamed it into the air, and then I heard His reply.

"Beloved."

Williams's eyebrow arched in skepticism, but Sienna just smiled.

"I know you're thinking I'd lost my mind. But I'm not making this up, William. I actually heard the still, small voice of God above all of the chaos in my mind. I sat down and cried, really cried for the first time in months. You see, until that moment I'd been afraid that if I started crying, I'd never stop. Oh, I shed a few tears here and there, but to purge myself? To weep and rage until I couldn't move anymore and then just start again? Never, not me. I've battled depression all of my life and knew if I started crying, I'd never stop."

"I never knew you battled with depression."

Sienna saw the tenderness in his eyes and smiled, a tiny trembling of lips which didn't quite reach her eyes. "There's a lot that people don't know about me. I've been very good at hiding the real me. But no more. If someone doesn't like the real me, it's their loss."

He squeezed her hand. "So, what happened after you heard the still, small voice of God calling you 'beloved'?"

Sienna took a sip of her coffee to gather her thoughts. She'd told this story only once to her church family and never realized how hard it would be to tell it again—especially to a skeptic. "Well, I'd like to say just hearing His voice made everything all better, but that's not true. I was so angry with God. I just couldn't let go. Not yet. We had a screaming match."

Her words trailed off at the snicker he tried to muffle.

"I'm sorry." William gasped and fought the laughter bubbling up in his throat. "I just can't imagine God being so real that He'd actually talk, much less engage in a screaming match with you."

A slight shake of her head preceded Sienna's words. "Well, actually I did all the screaming. God just whispered."

"Whispered what?"

"I asked Him why? He answered, 'Beloved' and 'My love is sufficient.'

"I asked, 'what's the point?' He answered, 'Love bears all things, believes all things, hopes all things, endures all things. Love never fails.'

"I really let Him have it then, shaking my fist at the sky and arguing that love does fail. I demanded to know where He was when Jace and Olivia lay trapped beneath the wreckage, suffocating in their own blood." Sienna paused and took another sip of her coffee. Her hand shook, voice trembled. She took a deep breath and continued.

"Then He told me that He had plans for me. Plans for hope and a future. Of course, I couldn't see past the pain in my present to even consider the future, and I told Him so. I told Him they were my life, my hope and my future and He'd let them die."

This time William's snort of disbelief halted her words. "Your life and hope? Not from what I hear. That may be true about the baby. But from what I understand, your husband was a real jerk and you're probably better off without him."

An angry flush warmed her cheeks. She narrowed and hardened her gaze as she considered her next words which were spoken between teeth clenched as tightly as the fists in her lap. "It's true Jace wasn't the best of men. Second choice husbands usually aren't. But that doesn't mean I wanted him dead."

Her meaning wasn't lost on him. The memory of her pleading with him to marry fresh out of high school rose like a thundercloud between them. William squirmed, swallowed hard, and then lifted his cup in mock salute.

"Touché. Please continue your story."

Not sure if she wanted to say another word, Sienna swallowed the lump in her throat and lifted her water glass with a trembling hand to take a sip. Silence stretched between them. Tense. Wary.

William reached across the table and lifted her chin with his finger. "Sienna, I'm sorry. True or not, my comment was way out of line. I'd really like to know what happened after you had your screaming match with God."

Uncomfortable with confrontation on every level, Sienna pushed aside the negative emotions the moment evoked and continued in the same soft voice she'd started with. "After I said what I did about them being my future, He simply whispered, 'beloved,' again. That's when I broke down and cried for what seemed like hours. Afterward, I asked Him to show me how or even why I should want to start over."

"What happened then?" William couldn't keep quiet. Despite the tension that had risen between them, the tale engrossed him as no other had. Everything about her convinced him what she experienced was real, and he wanted to know more—about God, and about the woman she'd become.

"Sunlight burst through the clouds. A rainbow danced on the mist. A dove cooed as it settled on its nest. Children's laughter rang on the wind."

He frowned. "That's it? No thundering voice? No warm, fuzzy feelings? No epiphany?"

Harshness forgotten Sienna grinned. "No, only a revelation. You see, those are all sights and sounds of life. Of love. In those few moments I knew and understood, what God wanted of me. He wanted me to live, to hope, and to love. For where there is love, God is forever present. His love is perfect. Perfect love which casts out the deepest of darkness. I guess you could say that *was* my epiphany."

He noted the way her entire being lit up with conviction; felt it all the way to his core. And just like that I'm forgiven, he thought. The realization touched his heart as no sermon ever had. "So, what did you do then?"

"I wept again, only this time they were tears of gratitude and hope. I threw the pistol away, turned away from the darkness in my soul which had overtaken my life and headed toward the light–the light of Christ–the light of life."

"So that's it? No more doubts, no more fears, just you and God, happy ever after?"

Heads turned when her laughter rang out in the coffee shop. Smiles bloomed on harried faces.

Sienna wiped tears of hilarity off her cheeks, surprised and glad she'd withstood the pain of telling her story as well as the quick flash of anger and could emerge from both with renewed hope. "Oh yes, plenty of each. But William, the bible teaches us that we can choose how we live. In Deuteronomy God said, 'I've put before you, life and death...therefore, choose life.' When those doubts and fears rise up, I still have to choose to believe in His good plan for my life and my future."

"And have you any idea yet, what the future might hold?"

She nodded. "Love, peace, joy and hopefully another family one day."

"Is that what you really want?"

"More than anything else." She fidgeted under his scrutiny. "OK, enough about me. What about you, what do you want out of life?"

William's heart hammered in his chest when he realized her dreams coincided with his. Not until that moment did he comprehend how much he wanted someone to share his life with. Nor had he appreciated how much he wanted the kind of faith and optimism she exuded. He shrugged hoping she couldn't read his thoughts. "Guess I want the same things in life everybody else does... A decent place to live. Enough money to live comfortably. Someone to share it all with."

"So, what's stopping you, or has stopped you, from getting all you want?"

William sipped his now-cold coffee and grimaced. "This rat-race we call life. Sheer madness if you ask me."

Once again her laughter bubbled throughout the room. William watched in amazement as her contagious joy affected everyone around them. Businessmen, frustrated moms, and irritable children all responded. Heads turned. Furrowed brows smoothed. Frowns turned to smiles. His eyebrow quirked in curiosity. "What's so funny?"

Her laughter trailed off into giggles between words. "You. I never knew you were so pessimistic. I mean, you've always had those dark, brooding good looks. But a pessimist?"

"Dark, brooding good looks? Sounds like something out of a romance novel. Besides, I'm not a pessimist, I'm a realist."

"Oh please, realist my foot. You've been scowling since the moment you arrived nearly an hour ago. You probably had a frown on your face before you got here.

One, by-the-way, which deepened the moment you saw me. Like you'd seen a ghost."

Shocked because her words echoed his exact thoughts when he walked in and realized the woman he'd chatted with online was the same girl he'd known and loved as a teen, William flushed and scrambled for an explanation. "I was just surprised. I mean, Sienna is not that common a name, but I wasn't sure until I got here that it was really you."

Her merry hazel eyes danced with humor, but she simply arched an eyebrow at him without comment and rose from her chair. She held a hand toward him. "Come on, I know what we're going to do today."

He couldn't resist the lure of her joy, and grinned as he placed his hand in hers. "What are we going to do?"

"I'm going to show you the beauty and joy of life. If only for today."

Hope flared in his heart that she may be the one person who could do what he considered to be impossible. After all, he never really got over her. Nor did he forget how she'd touched his heart so many years ago in a way no one had since.

They paused at the door to fasten their jackets and slip on caps. She took his hand again and led him across the way and two blocks down to a park on the opposite side of the road. Holiday decorations still lined the streets and would remain well into the new year. Santa's sleigh, pulled by reindeer and loaded with packages took up an entire corner. A life-sized, wooden nativity occupied another. Draped with Christmas lights and more holiday décor, the tiny wooden bridge they traversed crossed over a creek and swayed under their feet. Sienna stopped midway to their destination. "Listen."

He cocked his head. "What?"

"What do you hear?"

He turned in the direction she gazed, stood still, and tried to hear what she heard. A smile tugged at his lips when he faced her once more. Her eyes were alight with joy.

"You hear it too, don't you?"

"Tell me what you hear, Sienna."

"Children laughing, the sounds of joy, of love. Two things that make this world go around are love and joy. A child's laughter encapsulates both."

His heart melted another degree. He slipped his arm around her waist, took her hand in his, and walked with her to a bench on the edge of the frozen pond where children ice skated in a flurry of color and movement. Never in his life had he felt as complete as he did in that moment.

"Do you skate?"

She nodded. "I love to. Olivia loved to also. Jace had two left feet when it came to skating and dancing."

"Well, I don't." He pulled her up with him. "Let's go."

They changed into rented skates and danced across the ice. Hours later, weak from laughter, giddy with excitement, they shared soup and salad at a nearby restaurant.

"What's next on your agenda for showing me the beauty and joy of life?"

Sienna shivered. "After we thaw out a bit, we'll walk back to where our cars are parked, fetch mine and… you'll just have to wait and see."

"I must warn you: I don't like surprises."

"I love surprises. They're what make life interesting."

As much as she had known in her heart the person she'd chatted with online was the same boy she fell in love with in high school–and somewhere deep inside still loved–Sienna never dreamed they would actually spend a whole day together. Just as she had known twenty years ago, she felt from the very depths of her soul they were meant to be together. Now, she hoped the afternoon would melt into evening and linger. Where could they go? What could they do that would surpass the last few hours spent skating with children? A thought wormed its way into her mind. An image formed. Idea gelled.

She finished her allotted one glass of wine and excused herself to depart to the ladies room. She returned to find William ready to leave. He held the jacket for her to slip on, then took her hand in his and linked arms with her.

"Where to?"

"We'll get my car and go for a drive." Once ensconced in the warmth of her economy sized SUV, the atmosphere nice and toasty, she headed out of the city.

"Any place special you're taking me?"

She laughed. "Yep. Just relax, William and enjoy the drive."

The atmosphere grew comfortable as they rode in silence. Sienna wondered if he was immersed in the same pleasant memories which warmed her. She glanced over at him and remembered with profound clarity the way she felt the first time his electric blue eyes met hers in high school. The thrill that raced through her every time their hands brushed. The pain of losing him when he said they were too young to fall in love. Her heart beat in wild jubilation that this might be a second chance at her life-long dream of marriage and children.

She slipped an instrumental CD in the disc drive and turned the volume down to where the music served as a backdrop for the scenery which unfolded before and around them. A rainbow shimmered in the sky off to the east. Clouds surrounded mountain peaks like halos to the north and west. As the car climbed upward, small waterfalls burst through rocks to splash onto the road. Icicles hung like crystal prisms and reflected sunlight in bursts of color in the air.

He reached over and took her hand in his, played with her fingers then kissed the tips. "You're right, this is beautiful. I guess I don't take time often enough to soak in the magnificence of everything around me."

A swarm of excitement tightened her stomach at his touch. Sienna sucked in a soft breath. Exhaled slowly. "That's the problem with most people today. They're all caught up in the rat race, as you so colorfully put it, that they don't appreciate the simple gifts God has given us."

She stopped at a roadside vantage point on the edge of a small canyon. They disembarked and stood together where heaven and earth met in a glorious profusion of rock and sky. Sienna moved forward, leaned over the guardrail, and hollered, "Hello!" then burst into laughter when her voice echoed back in answer.

"Your turn."

William chuckled, shook his head, and took a step back.

"C'mon, loosen up a bit and have fun."

"I've had more fun so far today than I believe I've had in my entire life. Don't want to overdo it. Besides, being so close to the edge makes me nervous. So, back up will you?"

She cocked her head and eyed him, so handsome hunkered down in his jacket, his breath tiny wisps of fog in the chilly air. Flakes of pristine white snow clung to his dark hair, glimmered, and left a silky shine in their wake as they melted away. "So close to the edge of what, the mountain or falling in love... With life," she qualified as bubbles of heat burst beneath her skin.

William took her hand in his, raised it to his lips. "Both."

She laughed, twirled away from him, and challenged him to a race.

Her feet slipped on the icy walkway. He wrapped his arms around her waist and hauled her against him. He lowered his eyes to her lips which quivered only inches from his then looked up to capture her gaze in a heated embrace.

William's heart thundered in his chest. Breath clogged his throat. "Careful." His voice sounded raspy to his own ears. "To race on this ice is sheer madness."

Her eyes shone with laughter. She brushed her fingers through his hair and slid from his grasp. She hurried ahead of him and picked up a handful of snow then turned and began to walk backward.

"Sienna, don't you dare," he warned, no doubt in his mind what her plans were when she packed the snow into a firm ball.

She tossed the globe into the air, once, twice, as though considering the consequences. With a laugh she threw it at him and made a mad dash for the SUV. She wasn't fast enough to escape retaliation when he scooped up a handful and slung it in her direction. Giggles trailed on the breeze and danced straight into his soul. He found himself laughing while they pummeled each other with snowballs and realized he was falling in love with her all over again. Breathless, he held up his hands in defeat. "No more, I surrender."

Sienna threw one last bombshell, flung her arms open wide, and exclaimed to the heavens, "The earth declares the glory of the Lord."

She twirled in a circle then plopped onto the ground and proceeded to make a snow angel. William watched her for a moment then walked over to where she lay, her arms and legs moving in a scissor-like motion. "C'mon and make angels with me."

He held a hand toward her. "Why would I make angels of snow when I'm looking at one in the flesh?"

His words feathered over her like a caress and warmed her blood. Sienna halted her movements then took his outstretched hand and let him pull her to her feet. His arms wound around her. Hands brushed the snow from her back. He urged her closer to his hard frame and breathed her name as his lips covered hers in a sweet, tender gesture.

"Sienna, my sweet, to wallow in this is nothing short of madness. You could catch pneumonia or some other nasty ailment." He ran his hands through her hair then over her back and shoulders in an effort to chase the chill from her skin.

She smiled and caressed his cheek. "William, my dear, it behooves us to remember God gives His angels charge over us and to honor and acknowledge them. To not take advantage of an opportunity like this and create snow angels is what sheer madness is."

He chortled. "C'mon. My turn to pick our destination. Give me the keys, and I'll drive."

Sienna handed him her keys and climbed into the passenger side of her vehicle while he walked around and slid behind the steering wheel. Within moments, they sat in toasty warmth and chatted amiably as William made his way down the mountain and through the valleys to the west. The sun slid below mountain peaks. Its golden hue changed the pristine white to rich cream in its descent from the sky. The moon rose in all its glory. Stars twinkled on in the heavens and guided their way back to where he'd parked his car.

"I'll pick you up in two hours."

"Can I at least have a hint on where we're going?"

William shook his head. "My turn to surprise you."

"But what do I wear? At least tell me if I should dress casual or formal."

William had no idea if the black-tie charity gala he always attended on New Year's Eve and to which he had tickets for, would surpass the beauty of the day, but he doubted she would be disappointed. "Formal."

Less than two hours later he stood on her porch and waited for her to open the door. When she did, he thought he'd surely die from lack of oxygen in the way she left him breathless.

The emerald gown accentuated her tiny form and transformed her hazel eyes into a brilliant green. Her hair, pulled up at the crown with a diamond clasp fell in ringlets over her shoulders and down her back. If she wore makeup at all, the application was flawless and added a translucent sheen to her creamy complexion.

Unable to speak past the breath backed up in his lungs, William whispered, "wow."

She laughed and took his arm then let him escort her to the waiting limousine.

They dined and danced for hours. He waltzed her through the open doors onto the balcony. The clear, star filled sky provided a gorgeous backdrop to the music trailing them. William knew he'd remember this day for the rest of his life. The clock struck midnight.

He twirled her back into the ballroom. "How does it feel to be the most beautiful woman in this place?"

"Like Cinderella at the ball."

"Cinderella couldn't hold a candle to you, sweet Sienna. Not a star in the heavens can outshine the light in you. What do you say we fly down to Vegas, get married, and continue the new year as husband and wife?"

Her laughter sparkled through the room like fairy dust and created magic in its wake. Smiles bloomed. More laughter followed. Even the music seemed brighter.

"I'd say that's madness, dear William, sheer madness. Let's do it!"

The End

Dear Reader,

First Corinthians 13 says that LOVE bears all things, believes all things, hopes all things, endures all things, and never fails. We've all experienced the loss of loved ones and one thing I can say, without a doubt, is that faith in God, and the faithfulness of God, will work miracles in your life if you open your heart and release your grief.

If you don't know Him already, I pray that you will seek the Lord Jesus Christ and if you do, that you will pursue a closer walk with Him.

As always may God BLESS and keep you and yours in the palm of His mighty hand!

Love Un-Masked

Kelli Tremonte ran trembling hands through her hair, wrapped the locks around her fingers and resisted the urge to pull and scream.

Or break down and cry.

Another year's come and gone and I'm no closer to overcoming this curse!

Most people wouldn't call shyness a curse. But for Kelli, the inability to effectively socialize had become just that. Which is why she began working with a Life Coach two months ago.

Smoothing her hair, she prayed this last ditch effort to eradicate her personality disorder would be the one to actually work and knocked on Cody Smith's door. Tiny bubbles of heat burst beneath her skin when he opened it with a flourish and ushered her in.

"So, how did the week go?"

That smile. That voice. Her heart did a slow swirl into her stomach.

Kelli fidgeted in her chair and cleared her throat before detailing the week past. "I don't know what I'm doing wrong!" She all but wailed the admission. "I've tried everything we outlined. I don't have a lot of reasons to speak with my job as an ASL Interpreter, but I tried to create opportunities."

"Be patient with yourself. Change is progressive and every little victory is something to celebrate. Let's focus on the good."

They spent the next hour reframing what she

deemed disappointment in a positive light.

"So, what do you think a next step might be?"

Kelli shrugged.

Cody flipped through his calendar. "There's a masked Mardi Gras Ball next week. Why don't you plan to attend? Perhaps speaking will become easier if you feel less exposed. In fact, there are several events over the next few weeks that present perfect opportunities to put yourself out there without really being 'out there' so to speak."

Excitement curled in the pit of her stomach. Maybe Cody was right! Mardi Gras might be the easiest way for her to get comfortable associating with members of the opposite sex, especially since she could pretend to be someone else. Memories of playing dress-up as a child reminded her of a time when she wasn't afraid to say what was in her heart.

Oh, to connect with that little girl again.

"Guess I need to find a costume shop."

His chuckle set a kaleidoscope of butterflies bouncing off her ribcage.

If everyone were as easy to talk to as Cody, I'd have no problems whatsoever. The thought hummed along her senses. They scheduled her next appointment for after the ball, and she left with firm resolve to be free of her malady by Fat Tuesday.

Overcoming a lifetime Tof timidity in eight weeks might not seem plausible to some, but for the first time in a long time, Kelli decided to believe in miracles and magic instead of impossibilities. She spent the rest of the afternoon shopping for costumes then mapped out a plan of action to implement in her quest to break free. She even called Cody, voiced her commitment aloud, and rescheduled her appointment for the day after Ash Wednesday.

By the time Twelfth Night arrived Kelli actually anticipated her adventure. A valet escorted her to the door where she was met by a dashing figure of royalty who offered his arm as though he'd awaited her arrival alone. He twirled her into the ballroom and within moments they were engaged in exhilarating conversation. Something about him felt familiar but with his voice muffled by the mask, she couldn't quite place him.

Kelli thrilled at how easy it was to mix, mingle and converse with the other attendees, but no matter how many times she and her new friend parted ways to do so, they always ended up in each other's arms. As the evening dwindled, they promised to meet at the next ball and gave hints about their costume, so they'd be sure and find each other.

Time flew by as it usually does when you're having fun. Kelli blossomed throughout Mardi Gras season so much that she nearly cancelled her final session with Cody. Her prince, as she'd come to know him, encouraged her to follow through and finish what she'd started with her Life Coach, especially since the success she'd had over the past weeks flowed into her everyday life.

It seemed as though each life skill she'd learned and

practiced so far – prayer, meditation, affirmations – fell into place. She felt free, unencumbered and her social life had bloomed.

Kelli arrived for her appointment with Cody. A spark of recognition shivered over her skin when he opened the door, his face partially covered by an intricate design. His grin and tone of voice when he bid her 'hello,' eradicated the last shadow in her heart. She smiled and reached for his hand. "No more masks."

The End

Dear Reader,

I hope you enjoyed this brief romantic story. Like Kellie, many of us have something we're afraid to face, to overcome. For me, that's old mindsets of lack, fear, and poverty.

How do we change something we've entertained our entire life? As Cody suggests by reframing those thoughts and ideas into a more positive light. Prayer and meditation as well as affirmations, written and spoken, work wonders also. After all, faith comes by hearing... Especially hearing your own voice speaking words of life over your circumstances.

The Bible teaches us in Proverbs 23:7 "as a man thinks therefore he is." And we've all heard sermons and songs extolling... "Let the weak say I am strong. Let the poor say I am rich," etc. So, make a recording on your phone or computer of affirmations for changing your thoughts and reprogramming your mind. Meditate on them daily and watch your life change!

If you don't know HIM already, I pray you will seek a personal relationship with the Lord, Jesus Christ and if you do, that you'll continue to draw closer to Him and in all things you will give Him praise.

Meanwhile, I wish ALL of you, sweet friends, to be blessed with an overwhelming increase of God's almighty good.

Until next time, take care, God Bless and Remember: *Change starts within so be the change you want to see in the world.*

Choices

Camie waited to be escorted to her seat. Her heart throbbed with excitement. Country Music superstar Kip Allen has come home!

Everyone ranted and raved about the homegrown country boy who had made it big— three albums in five years, all gold. Camie remembered the shy, humble guy with rusty-gold hair and sea-green eyes who came to life when he had a guitar in his hands.

Her mind wandered back to high-school days and the many times he could be found on the outdoor patio where students congregated during lunch and break times. Strumming his guitar, and crooning a song, with girls gathered around him like bees to a hive.

Now look. The little amphitheater which usually hosted a live radio broadcast of French music and humor was packed wall-to-wall with people who'd watched Kip grow up and then make it to the Big Time.

He'd been on the road for more than a year during his *Home is Where the Heart is* tour—even had flown his parents out to meet him at Thanksgiving and Christmas, but his final performance was here, in his hometown of Eunice, Louisiana on Valentine's Day. Perfect ending to the tour, Camie mused, if home truly is where his heart is.

The lights dimmed. She sat mesmerized when he appeared on stage and began to croon one love song after another, mixing in a few boot-stomping hits. Words she knew intimately.

Too soon, the concert ended, and security officers rushed her backstage. Waiting in the shadows apart from the throng of frenzied fans vying for autographs and pictures, she watched with concern as Kip raked his fingers through his hair. He heaved a tired sigh, insisted on no more autographs, and then headed for his dressing room.

Camie stepped forward. "Just one more autograph?" Kip turned at her soft request. His eyes lit with recognition, and he gave her an unreserved smile.

"Camie!" He enfolded her in a big hug. "What are you doing back here?"

A flush warmed her skin at the husky baritone voice. "I won the prize package from the radio station. You know: Front row seat, backstage pass, autographed C.D., etcetera, etcetera, etcetera."

Her heart raced at his nearness; body trembled in his strong embrace. Feeling way too comfortable in his arms, she disentangled herself and took a step back.

He grinned. "Great. You look good."

Her heart skipped a beat. "So do you."

Electricity sizzled between them. Always had.

Even in high school.

Theirs had been a subtle romance, underscored by sensual currents that hummed whenever their eyes met or they ventured into a conversation, both too shy to take the relationship further.

"What ever happened to us?" She wondered aloud, finding it difficult to speak past the heart hammering in her throat. "I still get tongue-tied when you're near."

He smiled, that lazy, heart-stopping grin that drove females from age five to fifty into a frenzy and pulled her close once more. "You do?"

The seductive tone of his voice sent delicious shivers down her spine. Camie choked on a yes.

"Me too." He stroked her cheek.

Her senses swirled at the tender touch. She placed her hand over his and gazed into his sea-green eyes. Whether a moment, an eternity, or the simple span of a heartbeat passed, she wasn't sure, but she relished the encounter. He dropped his hand from her face and broke eye contact.

"I don't know what happened. I wanted to roam. You wanted a home." He chuckled at the corny rhyme. "Sounds like the makings of a hit."

Camie shook her head. He was right. They'd dreamed different dreams, wanted different things. But somehow their destinies were entwined. Their lives paralleled each other more than he knew. "Want to go for a cup of coffee or a cold drink?"

He brought his attention back to her face. Once again, she was unable to pull her eyes away from his hypnotic gaze.

"I'd love to. But where? There's no place I can go and not be mobbed. You'd think I wouldn't be such a big deal here, in my hometown."

Camie heard the tension and fatigue in his voice. "How about my place? I have a nice, quiet home in the country."

The look in his eyes warmed her all over, but Camie

had news for him—the invitation was not a come-on. Ignoring the limousine surrounded by anxious fans, they dashed into the patrol car driven by her father.

"Hungry?" she asked, once her father had seen them safely inside her house.

"Starved." He took a step toward her, evidently no longer shy but confidently aware of his effect on women.

The look in his eyes left her breathless. She put a firm hand on his chest. Heat seeped through her palm, traveled up her arm and settled in a warm pool in her heart as his lips lowered toward hers. She managed—just barely—to turn her head so that his mouth brushed her cheek, knowing that if she allowed his kiss, she wouldn't be able to stop from losing herself in his arms.

"That's not why I brought you here, Kip. You may have changed over the years, but I haven't."

Though unable to mask the disappointment in his voice, Kip apologized. "I'm sorry. Guess I have changed. Stardom does that to you. Strips away the shyness and makes you confident."

"You mean, presumptuous? Arrogant? Conceited?"

He chortled. "That too."

A sheepish grin twisted his sensuous lips. The shy, humble boy was back, making him even harder to resist. Camie ached to touch him, to hold him and confess the love she held for him. Mentally shaking herself, she stepped out of his reach and dispelled the tension with a smile. "How about pizza? Like the one we made in Home Economics class?"

"Sounds great," Kip answered, glad that he hadn't

offended her to the point of being thrown out. Especially considering the fact that he had no idea where they were or how he'd get back to town if she did.

In the hours that ensued, they cooked and cleaned, laughed, and talked. Reminiscing over the years and remembering how much they had in common. Regretting the time lost, goals unmet, and dreams unfulfilled.

"So, how come you're not married?"

"The right man hasn't come along yet."

He grinned. "Still looking for your knight in shining armor?"

She shrugged. Shyness colored her cheeks. A quiet light emanated from her, mesmerizing Kip. Her soft hazel eyes drew him in and looked deep into his soul like no other had—in high school where he met her, or since.

"Hope springs eternal, I guess." Kip wondered why he suddenly felt so hopeless, so bereft, as though something was lost or missing. *Something precious.*

An awkward silence rose between them. He watched the emotions play across her features. She glanced down, closed her eyes.

"I know he'll come around when the Lord is ready for him to."

Her voice was soft, barely audible, but he heard. He raised his eyebrow in amusement when she bit her lip and color flamed her face. Evidently, she had not meant to speak aloud.

Kip grinned. The remark was so like her. His Camie. Sweet. Innocent. Trusting. Faithful. He brushed his knuckles across her cheek in a tender gesture and resisted the urge to gather her close and cover her lips with his. He'd overstepped his boundaries once and didn't dare make the mistake a second time.

His Camie. It had been a long time since he thought of her in that way. Quite a while since he thought of her at all, he realized with a pang of sadness and guilt. Once upon a time she was *all* he thought about, and his biggest dream was to make her his.

Heart aching, he rose from his seat and walked to the door as the clock chimed five. Opening it, he stepped onto the porch. Gazing eastward, he anticipated the sunrise. They'd talked all night, but he'd never felt better or more alert.

The sun broke over the horizon brightening the sky by degrees. Luminous shades of blue—midnight, indigo, azure—then cobalt, sapphire, pale. Fingers of yellow and gold reached out to caress the clouds, turning them from gray to pink, then peach to brilliant orange. Kip took a deep, cleansing breath. "This is so peaceful, so wonderful. Seems like forever since I saw the sun rise from anywhere but a bus window or a hotel room."

He turned back to face her, his heart wistful. "I don't get to relax like this too often. Thank you."

Camie smiled, stretched languidly, and then walked to his side. He turned once more to watch the sky.

"You're welcome. Anytime. How about sunrise services at church? When was the last time you did that?"

He heaved a breath. "Been a long time since I attended church at all."

"I know." Sadness laced her soft voice.

"It's hard, Camie," he confessed, unable to meet her eyes. Standing next to her made him acutely aware of how low he'd actually slumped. How far he'd backslidden. Conscience made him try to explain it away. "The parties, the road, and a dozen different cities in twice as many days."

The explanation sounded empty and hollow even to his ears. *Exactly like the excuse it is.* Pride was a bitter pill to swallow in light of the truth. Kip blinked back tears and forced the hard lump down his throat.

"I'm tired. Physically. Mentally. Emotionally."

"Spiritually?" The question held no accusation.

Kip shrugged, gritted his teeth, and fought the urge to break down and sob. He nodded.

"Quit. Or take a break."

"Wish it were that simple."

"It can be." She ran a hand down his back in a subtle caress, and then quickly crossed her arms over her chest.

Her soft voice offered quiet assurance. The flames of hope curling in his heart at her touch were crushed at her sudden withdrawal. Kip's heart ached as possibilities collided with cold reality. "You don't understand. It's hard to stay at the top once you get there. You've got to be out there with the fans."

Never realized how lonely it is at the top.

"I understand a whole lot more than you know. Have you ever heard of Kameron Skye or Skip Cameron?"

"The songwriter and the novelist? Sure, Skip's one of my favorite writers. I've recorded several of his songs.

Never met the guy though. They say he's a hermit. Just sends in his music and collects his checks. And Kameron Skye, man she's great. Three novels in five years and her first book is still on the top ten lists. I'll never forget when one of the back-up singers bought it." He laughed at the memory.

"'Kameron Skye' sounds more like something you look at than a real person," he mused, turning his gaze southwest, toward Cameron, Louisiana. Kip considered his words a full minute before continuing. "But her writing is brilliant, different. Not just ordinary romance but love and faith and hope. She mixes all of those things together with real life situations and creates a best seller every time. I get a lot of song ideas by reading her work."

"Thank you. I've never received a more beautiful compliment."

His eyebrows shot up in surprise. He turned to face her. "You're Kameron Skye?"

She nodded. "And Skip Cameron."

"You're kidding!" He was unable to hide the surprise and disbelief in his voice. Camie merely eyed him, a delicate lift to her brow.

"How do you do it?"

"Do what, avoid the hype?" She shrugged and then paused as if choosing her words with care. "It's all in the choices you make, Kip. You chose to roam. I chose a home. Both of our dreams have come true. I just have more peace with mine."

He looked around, noting for the first time the simple elegance of his surroundings. "You don't live like a best-selling author and songwriter."

"True happiness doesn't come from materialistic wealth." She smiled. "Now, we've got to hurry if we're going to get to church in time for sunrise services."

The early morning Mass was beautiful in the little country church. Sunlight streamed in through the stained-glass windows, creating tiny bursts of rainbows on the walls and floors.

Kip reflected on his life over the past eight years, thankful for all he had. Hopeful for all he wanted. Realizing with stark clarity everything he'd missed out on. After Mass, a heavy stillness surrounded them as they made their way to his parents' home.

"I want to tell you something." Camie broke the silence when she turned into the driveway, knowing that this might be her one, her only, chance to reach him with the truth. Taking a deep breath, she sent a quick, silent prayer that she was making the right choice in opening her heart to him.

"I had a dream not too long ago. An angel appeared and assured me that no prayer would go unanswered as long as I continue to keep the Lord as the center of my life. And faith the focus of my writing." Her eyes searched his, praying he understood what she was saying. Taking a gamble of the heart, she told him the rest. "Then the angel handed me a baby— a child with rusty-gold hair and sea green eyes— just like yours. The songs, the novels, they were all written with you in mind."

He reached out and brushed a strand of hair off her face in a gentle caress, but his expression told her that he had no idea of the depth of what she said. Or how much it cost her to say it. After a moment of silence, he feathered his lips over hers and got out of the car.

Camie blinked back tears all the way home. She'd planted the seed. It was up to God to make it grow. She knew it wouldn't be easy. Kip would still have to perform. She'd still have to write. It was their gift, their calling. But she knew it could work. They could do it together. So, she had a room built, furnished it with the latest and greatest technology in recording sound, and continued to pray.

* * *

Kip hesitated. A full year had passed since his last visit with Camie. A long, dreadful year. An unsuccessful year. The struggles he'd had. The album he'd yet to finish. The tour he'd refused. Everything he'd done, every place he'd gone, the memory of their night together had haunted him. Chased his dreams, tortured his thoughts, and warmed his heart until peace could only be found in obedience and in returning home.

Though his parents had kept him abreast of local news, and he knew she wasn't married, he had no idea how Camie would react to him simply showing up on her doorstep. He glanced down at the gift he'd brought for her, then raised his eyes to the star studded sky and said a quick prayer. He turned back, knocked once, then a second time. "Camie!"

Camie struggled from a sound sleep to the thud of someone pounding on her door and calling her name.

She recognized his voice immediately. The voice she'd loved since high school. The same one that serenaded her daily and inspired her writing. Throwing a robe on, she raced to the foyer and flung open the door. She gasped, covering trembling lips with fingers just as shaky when Kip held out a rose.

He stepped forward and took her hand in his. "You were praying for me, weren't you? Well, your prayers have been answered, Camie. I hope you're not going to be disappointed."

Overcome with emotion, all she could do was shake her head, blink back tears, and force a quivering smile. She reached for the rose, its symbolism known only to her and the saint to whom she'd prayed for intercession with the Lord Jesus.

"I had a dream last night," Kip continued. "You were holding a baby. A child, with rusty-gold hair and hazel eyes. I love you, Camie. Always have. I've decided to come home for a while and to change my focus. You're the first person I wanted to see when I got into town."

The tears escaped, dripping down her cheeks as he said the words she had always wanted him to say.

"Welcome home," she whispered, as his arms wrapped around her, and his lips met hers in a kiss ripe with passion and the promise of tomorrow.

The End

Dear Reader,

For all of you long-time friends, it is my prayer that you enjoy my short stories as much as you do the novels. To my new friends, may these stories provide not only enjoyment but also entice you to *taste and see the goodness of the Lord* in reading my other works.

As we can see in this story, Camie and Kip had similar dreams but chose different paths. Every day we choose how we are going to live our lives. We can choose to be negative or positive, happy, or sad, content, or despondent. However, the Bible gives us examples of what we should choose. Deuteronomy 30:19 says... "I have set before you life and death... Therefore, choose life." Jesus said, "I am the way and the life, follow me."

If you don't know Him already, I pray that you will pursue a relationship with the Lord Jesus, and if you do, that you will continue to walk in the love of God—through Jesus and the abundant life He died to provide for you.

Remember... This **is your** choice.

As always, may God bless and keep you and yours in the palm of His mighty hand!

Casi's CPA

Casi MacGregor rubbed a dab of smoothing serum between her palms then ran a flat iron through her hair, taming the thick tresses into a stream of blonde silk that flowed down her back.

Excitement made her hand tremble, stomach flutter. She took a deep breath to calm the jitters and swiped on mascara, lip-gloss. Something big was bound to happen today. Casi knew and trusted her intuition well enough to recognize the signs–indicators which had appeared and built into a powerful sense of anticipation over the past few days.

She loved it when life handed her a surprise gift and all of her plans came together in a single moment of synchronicity. Like puzzle pieces that wouldn't fit one moment but slid perfectly into place the next. A laugh, deep, carefree, and full of joy bubbled through her lips.

"I love to hear that," her sister remarked as she walked into the room. "It's been so long since I've heard you laugh that way. I'm glad you're finding a bit of happiness."

The two stood together in front of the full-length mirror and smiled at their reflection. That they were twins could not be mistaken. Both wore similar outfits–khaki shorts, floral print blouses, strappy sandals. Shamrock earrings, necklaces and bracelets graced their bodice and arms. The only difference were the green streaks in her sister's blond hair to commemorate St.

Patrick's Day.

"Are you ready for the open house?"

Casi hugged Breanna. "Yes. You?"

Breanna's gaze travelled the room then settled back on her. "Yes. But if today goes well, we may need to hire additional staff."

Casi could tell by the hint of sadness in her sister's eyes she still missed the homes they'd left behind. But the changes they'd made while turning their great aunt's old Victorian into a brand new B&B had been a desperately needed venture after the arrest of their husbands seven years ago.

The joy in Casi's heart dimmed a bit, remembering those first years after her husband and brother-in-law had been convicted of Embezzlement and Federal Money Laundering. She felt a quick stab of pain remembering the grief, confusion, and fear as she and her sister struggled to rebuild lives torn apart by tragedy.

At first Breanna balked at the idea of turning their summer home on lakefront property into a place for strangers. But as their lives continued to unravel, the huge house had become more and more a safe haven. Besides, since the girls inherited the property it was all they had left after the government seized everything else. The fact that it was located in a whole other state gave them the opportunity to start over without the suspicion and distrust that haunted them back home.

"This was a great idea, Sis." Breanna's voice pulled Casi back into the present. "I know we didn't always see eye to eye, but I'm glad you talked me into it. Maybe now that things are settled, we can think about our future."

Casi shrugged. She had no desire to join the ranks of lonely women trolling the bars or online in search of a man. Unlike her sister whose faith and optimism allowed her to bounce back from adversity quite easily, it had taken years for Casi to grow from a sniveling victim into the strong, independent woman she now was. "If I'm meant to marry again, the perfect guy will show up when he's supposed to."

Breanna laughed and slipped her arm around Casi's waist. "Yeah, but not if he doesn't know where you are."

Casi brushed the familiar arguments away with a wave of her hand. "I'll be happy enough finding the right CPA before we're booked with reservations. I can handle simple bookkeeping, but I'd rather be in the kitchen or among the guests than crunching numbers."

Hooking her arm through Breanna's, Casi walked out of the room.

Her sister winked and grinned. "Me too. Who knows, you just might meet a tall, dark, handsome cowboy after all."

Casi rolled her eyes and groaned. "Heaven forbid. Besides, that's your dream, not mine."

Though the chance of meeting anything but a cowboy in the heart of Arizona is slim to none.

The two women walked from their cabin to the main house where people had already begun to gather and mingle then went their separate ways. The first thing Casi noticed in the sea of cowboy hats was the ball cap pulled low over his forehead as a man walked, no *strolled*, toward her. The second was his starched shirt tucked neatly into casual slacks. Although he wore boots, there was nothing cowboyish about this guy. Tiny bubbles of heat burst in her blood. Her heart did a slow waltz into her stomach.

Eyes the color of thunderclouds danced merrily behind his wire-framed lenses then swept over her in a gaze as potent as a caress. His lips quirked. "Heard you're looking for a CPA."

The End

Dear Reader,

A dear friend said I wrote excellent short stories. I pray that's true and that you enjoy this one.

How often do we find ourselves in situations not of our choosing in which we're not 100% happy only to find God's hand has been all over us and our circumstances from the very beginning?

I hope this story will remind you to look for the blessing in all things and to trust God for His wisdom, direction, and gifts in every situation in your life.

If you don't know HIM already, I pray you will seek a personal relationship with the Lord, Jesus Christ and if you do, that you'll continue to draw closer to Him and in all things you will give Him praise.

Lilies for Sandi

"Sandi?"

She clutched the phone to keep her hand from trembling. "Yes."

"Hey, look, I'm not going to be home as early as I thought. This project is taking longer, and the team wants to get together for practice this afternoon then hit the gym."

"What about dinner, Brett?"

"Don't worry about me. I'll grab something while I'm out. Don't want heavy meals anyway, you know. Not good for performance."

"But tonight's our night. I'm supposed to drop Candie at Mom's this afternoon and..." Her words trailed off as he cursed.

"Look, I said I'm sorry, OK! Can't you understand how important this is to me? Football is my dream, my life. I can't make the NFL, so this new league is my only hope."

Football. Sandi wiped a tear from her cheek and fought back sobs. "Well, be careful. I'll see you when you get home."

She disconnected the call before he could respond, tossed the phone aside and then burst into tears. *So, he considered* football *his life?* "Should have known that wouldn't change."

She and Brett met in college. She, a cheerleader, he a football star. Theirs was love at first sight. A wild explosion of light and color from the first moment their eyes met. Boy what a word, Sandi thought. *Explosive* described their relationship right down to the core. Brett was high strung, volatile, rough. As the only child of middle aged parents, getting what he wanted, when he wanted, had never been an issue. And he'd wanted Sandi.

She had wanted him, too. Still did. But their dreams were different. He wanted to play, and not just football. He always had an excuse not to be home or out with her... Work, building a home for someone else instead of designing one for them, a beer or two with the guys, working out at the gym or shooting hoops with his friends. He'd been ecstatic when the notice in the paper appeared about a new indoor football team being formed, and she'd seen less and less of him.

If that were even possible considering the few hours of attention he granted his family.

Somewhere deep inside, Sandi believed Brett really loved her. He just didn't know how to show it. He wasn't ready for the responsibility of marriage, or the commitment required in maintaining the kind of love she dreamed of.

* * *

Brett snapped his cell phone closed, shoved it into his pocket and banished the guilt trying to worm its way into his heart. From the moment he held a football in his hands, he lived, breathed, and dreamed of a professional career. Football had been the one constancy in his life, and the only *real* connection he had with his parents.

Mom and Dad both loved the game, and both were devastated when his college career was cut short by his relationship with Sandi. An unplanned pregnancy thrilled her and infuriated him. Still, he'd done what he thought was right. Quit school, married her, worked to provide for his wife and daughter.

And grew apart from his parents.

Oh, they loved their granddaughter. Candie was the apple of everyone's eye. But, even after two years, she was more of an obligation that kept Brett from his dream than a reason to give it up. But now, with the formation of a new team in his hometown, that dream was closer to reality than it had ever been. It didn't matter that the current 'team' consisted of a bunch of guys who had been gearing up for tryouts since the paper announced the city's intent to get involved with the league in hopes of reviving what the fans had lost when the state's team dissipated years ago.

Brett knew he'd still have to impress the organization's coaches and managers to make it past the first cut. He'd researched the North American Professional Indoor Football League and was duly impressed with both stats and pay scale. The fact that the league and team owners were big into community service and charity work was a huge incentive also. He'd always had a burning desire to help and serve others and had done what he could while growing up and in college. But all that changed when Sandi got pregnant.

He'd tried to talk her into giving the baby up for adoption. Not that he didn't want children someday. But *someday* meant later, after college and being drafted into the pros. When she refused so adamantly and threatened to leave and raise the baby on her own with no help or contact, he did as he was raised to do.

The familiar stirring of anger and frustration flooded him. *Why, God? Why did You let this happen when You knew the plans I had for my life?*

This time he couldn't stop the sharp stab of guilt. It wasn't God's fault he'd ignored biblical teachings and gave in to lusts of the flesh. Remorse welled up in his heart. He closed his eyes. "God, how many times do I have to say I'm sorry? When will You forgive me? When will I not feel this anger and frustration and learn to appreciate the blessing Sandi and Candie are?"

He didn't really expect an answer.

His coworker and fellow team-hopeful knocked on the open door of his office. "Got the plans ready for this next house?"

Brett nodded and handed over the blueprints. His heart lightened a bit at the thought of another Habitat for Humanity house he'd designed. At least part of his lifelong ambition was being met with his job as architect for the organization. Gratitude rose up within and he sent a silent *Thank You* to God. Not only did he design the homes and draw up prints, often he helped with the construction. Well, he had until the announcement came about the NAPIFL team. Now he spent all of his spare time at practice or the gym.

Joe stepped over to the drafting table and unrolled the plans. A low wolf whistle accompanied his praise.

"Wow, Brett, this is the best so far. Reasonable, too. The family will surely be thrilled and grateful for the added room this house will give them and their foster children."

The thought of those people who took in special needs children to raise and care for reminded Brett how blessed he was to have a healthy child. He bowed his head for a moment and let the gratitude rise up and ease the sting of frustration. He sent another heartfelt prayer of praise and thanksgiving heavenward. Joe rolled the plans back up and slid them into the cardboard tube, then turned and saluted Brett.

"See you at practice."

Brett nodded. "Think I'll run home for a bit first." He picked up roses on the way. Hopefully he could soothe the disappointment hanging over his relationship enough to keep his guilt and dissatisfaction at bay.

* * *

Sandi heard the door of their apartment open and turned in surprise as Brett walked in. "I thought you were going to the gym and practice."

He held a dozen roses toward her. "I am. Just thought I'd drop by for a minute first."

Sandi took the roses, buried her nose in them and inhaled the heady scent. Hope trickled through the disappointment in her soul. "These are lovely. Thank you."

She raised her head to smile at him. Relief shadowed the love she hoped to see in his eyes. Sandi cocked her head. "Brett?"

A million unanswered questions hung in that single syllable.

Brett's smile was tentative. "I know I haven't been the best husband or father. I really don't know how to be either."

"Then why did you marry me?"

He shrugged. "Because it was the proper thing to do."

What little hope she felt died a quick, painful death. "I don't understand."

His eyes flashed with pain and regret.

"Neither do I, but it's time for some honesty between us. I do love you, Sandi, and our daughter. But the timing is all wrong for this, for us, for a family. I feel as though we've been living on broken dreams and false expectations. Just going through the motions. I don't know what to do, or how to fix it." He glanced at his watch, swore softly.

"I really need to run. We'll talk later." He brushed a kiss across her cheek, turned and fled.

Sandi fought the urge to throw the flowers at him as the door banged in his wake. She closed her eyes and let the emotions roll through her. "God, what does all this mean? What am I supposed to do?"

Brett's words bounced around her mind and echoed through the house. She got her answer. Sandi laid the roses on the table, packed a bag for her daughter and herself, then left.

** * **

Brett arrived home surprised to find Sandi gone. No note, no explanation. Nothing. Just gone. The acute emptiness and stark silence screamed obscenities at him. The roses he'd brought lay on the table, dying of thirst. He picked them up, and walked over to the trash can.

Don't.

The command reverberated so strongly in his spirit he hesitated. Anger surged through him.

"Why not?" he muttered and reached toward the trashcan.

Don't.

Again, the command resonated in his heart. Brett laid the flowers on the counter and dug a vase out of the cabinet then retrieved a pair of scissors from the junk drawer.

"OK, Lord, I don't know what You're trying to show me here," he mumbled. His voice sounded strange even to his own ears. He dropped an aspirin into the vase and filled it with water then trimmed each stem with meticulous precision before placing them in the container. Oddly, the chore soothed the turbulent emotions in his heart and mind. He placed the arrangement on the windowsill, cleaned up the snips of flower stalk and petals that had fallen, and then wiped the counter and table with a damp dishcloth.

Afterward, he dug around in the refrigerator and made a sandwich then poured a huge glass of milk and sat at the table.

Alone.

The clock on the wall struck midnight. He rinsed his dishes and placed them in the sink, unloaded his gym bag, took a shower, and then crawled into bed.

Alone.

The next morning, he rose, stumbled into the kitchen, and poured a cup of coffee. The cold, bitter brew tasted like ashes. *Yesterday's coffee.* He cursed and dumped the contents into the sink.

In the moments it took Brett to empty and rinse the coffee pot and filter container, he recognized he was way out of his league.

He had no clue how to make a pot of coffee.

"Can't be that hard." The petulance in his muttered comment echoed in the air.

The silence mocked him.

He cursed again and then filled the pot half full of water and poured it into the reservoir. He dug around in the cabinets and pantry until he found the filters, then searched the contents of every canister until he uncovered the coffee. A deep, appreciative whiff of the fragrant grounds gave him the courage to scoop some and place them in the filter. He snapped the filter basket closed and hit the button to turn on the machine.

Within moments, the aroma of fresh brewed java filled the air. He pumped his fist in triumph and poured a cup the minute the contraption stopped gurgling liquid into the pot. He eyed the thick fluid, sniffed, and felt a quick jolt of alarm. He took a cautious sip.

It tasted like sludge.

Brett shuddered and once again dumped the contents of his cup into the sink. A steady stream of curses flowed through the house as he stomped into the bedroom, tugged on clothes and shoes, and threw things into his gym bag.

He left the house and stopped at the first coffee shop he spotted, slammed out of the truck, and trudged inside. Grateful there wasn't a long line of desperate coffee drinkers ahead of him, he waited. Someone tapped him on the shoulder. Brett turned and came face to face with his coach.

"Morning."

"Hi, Coach."

"Why so glum?"

"No coffee yet this morning."

A flash of disbelief clouded the coach's eyes.

"Is that all?"

The line moved. Conversation halted. Brett stepped up to the counter, made his selection from the extravagant menu, and ordered. "And whatever my friend here wants," he told the perky blonde and stood aside to wait for coach to order. Once they received the drinks, the two moved off to a booth in a corner of the dining area.

Seated, coach took a sip of the hot brew then put down the cup. "Brett, I try to help my players in any way possible. If you need advice or just an ear, I'm always available."

Brett knew coach was a deeply spiritual man. He sipped his double espresso mocha latte and sighed. Part pleasure, part irritation. "Why is it when one aspect of your life seems to look up, another starts falling apart?"

When coach remained silent, Brett took another sip. "Wife walked out last night. No note, nothing."

"Y'all have a spat?"

"Marriage hasn't been all that great from the beginning. My fault, I know, but I can't seem to get a handle on my anger and disappointment for having to get married in the first place."

Coach's eyebrow shot up in question.

Brett leaned back in his chair and scrubbed a hand over his face. "Typical jock/cheerleader scenario—she got pregnant, yada, yada, yada. Guess the strain is just too much to bear anymore."

"Have you spoken to her since last night?"

Brett shook his head. "That's just it, I don't know whether to feel guilty or relieved now that she has left."

A flash of sympathy lit coach's gaze. Brett waited while the man sipped his coffee, anticipating his advice. Or judgment.

Coach put down the cup, smiled. "Anger and disappointment have a way of obscuring our blessings. My advice is to not make any rash decisions and to use this separation as a time of personal and spiritual growth." He glanced at his watch and rose. "Guess I'll see you at practice this afternoon."

Brett nodded. "Thanks, Coach."

When the man had exited the coffee shop, Brett ordered another coffee and a bran muffin, polished off the snack and then left for the gym.

* * *

Sandi slid into a booth at the local burger joint and waited for her best friend of a lifetime to arrive. Although distant cousins, the two women shared a bond most sisters didn't enjoy. It was as though God had created one spirit, carved it in half, and sent them into the world separate, yet together. He then blessed them doubly by placing them amongst blood relatives who lived in the same town.

Born three days apart, Karla and Sandi had attended the same school, occupied the same class rooms while growing up, and went to the same college for similar degrees. Sandi's education was cut short by pregnancy. Karla obtained her degree in Graphic Design and now owned and operated her own freelance business in that field.

Sandi smiled and stood as the slim, dark haired, dark eyed beauty walked through the door. Karla enfolded Sandi in a hug so tight, she thought she'd never catch her breath. They sat.

Karla reached out her hand. "So, what's going on now?"

Sandi blinked back tears. "Same old thing. Brett's more interested in football than his family. Although he did bring me roses last night."

"Really?"

Karla's sarcasm wasn't lost on Sandi. She nodded. "Yeah, he handed me a beautiful bouquet of mixed roses, right before telling me that he married me out of obligation and felt like we were just going through the motions of life as a couple."

Karla's eyes narrowed. Her hand knotted into a fist on the table. "Did you shove them up his…"

She bit off the comment, visibly struggling against saying more, then rolled her eyes heavenward with a remorseful sigh. "I'm sorry, Lord. He just makes me so angry! So, what did you do with the roses?"

"They're probably still lying on the table where I put them before I left."

Karla's eyebrow arched in surprise. "You left him?"

Tears pricked her eyes again. Sandi blinked them back. "I don't know what to do anymore, Karla. He did say he loves us…"

"But?"

Sandi shrugged. "But according to him, the timing is all wrong."

Karla snorted. "He should have thought of all that before he pursued you so ardently. I swear, with guys it's all about the chase!"

Sandi sighed. "Don't blame it all on him. I didn't run too hard or fast. I never understood what he saw in me anyway."

"Don't you dare give me that! You're beautiful and smart." Karla's eyes narrowed. "Do you think he has been, or is being unfaithful?"

Sandi thought for a moment then shook her head. "As far as I know, he hasn't."

"But you can't be completely sure he isn't. He's

always been surrounded by women, had his pick of the litter, so to speak."

"I'd like to think he has more respect for me, and himself, than to do something like that. If you could call football a mistress, then I'd definitely say he's unfaithful. He works all day and spends most of the evenings and weekends at the gym or at football practice."

"Anything that comes between a man and his wife and family is deserving of the title as far as I'm concerned. I'm glad you left. Let him fend for himself for a while. He'll figure out soon enough what he's missing."

Tears welled up in Sandi's eyes again, spilled over, and the deepest fears in her soul poured forth to the one person she knew would understand. "That's just it. What if he doesn't miss us? What if he'd rather be alone than with Candie and me, or someone else comes along who does nothing but stroke his ego? What am I going to do then? How can I compete with that?"

Empathy lit Karla's dark eyes. She reached for Sandi's hand.

Sandi sniffed. Her voice lowered to a helpless whisper. "I love him. Why doesn't he love me, Karla? What am I lacking? Why aren't I good enough?"

"I hate what's happened to you! You're beautiful and talented and smart, yet you've wrapped yourself so tightly around him that you have no self-esteem or confidence left. I'll tell you what you're going to do. You're going to work on healing your life, your soul, and your self-image. And you're going to finish your degree. If Brett Edwards is God's gift to you and not your gift to yourself, he'll come back, and you two will be stronger than ever. If not, you're better off without him."

Sandi's cell phone rang. She pulled it out of her pocket. Brett's name flashed on the screen. Before she could answer, Karla jerked it out of her hand and sent the call straight to voicemail.

"What'd you do that for?"

A sneer curled Karla's lip. "You haven't even been gone forty eight hours. Let him wonder where you are, what you're doing, and who you're with."

Sandi locked gazes with her cousin. "You forget we have a child together. I at least need to let him know she is OK."

She covered Karla's hand with hers. "I know you're angry with him for what you feel is a gross injustice on my behalf, but it takes two to tango, Karls. I love you for your loyalty and, you are right, I *do* need to rebuild my life, so it is not centered on Brett and his dreams. I'm counting on you to help me do that. But understand he will always be a part of my life, even if only as Candie's father. In the very least, he deserves respect for that. Your anger may be justified, but petty vengeance is not."

Karla had the grace to look sheepish, and guilty. She handed the phone back to Sandi. "You're right. I'm sorry."

Sandi took the phone, gave Karla's hand a squeeze then returned Brett's call. He answered on the third ring.

"Hello?"

"Sorry I missed your call."

"Where are you?"

"I decided to spend the weekend with my family."

"So, you'll be back sometime tonight?"

Sandi's heart fluttered at the glum tone. "Is that what you want, Brett? Last night you said you felt like we've just been going through the motions, and you married me out of obligation. Are you telling me you don't feel that way now?"

His sigh spoke volumes. Her heart plummeted. "You said it's time for some honesty between us. Be honest with me now. Do you *want* me and our daughter to come home?"

He hesitated and Sandy imagined him, head down, eyes closed, pinching the bridge of his nose, and/or fiddling with his cap, as he did when pushed for an answer he didn't have or wasn't ready to give. A heavy sigh preceded his words.

"I didn't ask you to leave, but as long as you have, maybe we should take some time apart and figure out where we're at, where we're going, and what we want out of life and our relationship."

Her sharp intake of breath lodged in her chest like a tight fist around her heart. "Fine. I'll come by Monday while you're at work and pick up a few things for Candie and me."

She disconnected the call before he could respond, then buried her face in her hands, unable to stem the tears this time. She heard Karla slide out of her side of the booth and welcomed the strong embrace as sobs tore from her in painful torrents. "He doesn't want us back."

"What exactly did he say?"

"He said since *I* decided to leave *him* maybe we should take some time apart and figure out what we want out of life and our relationship."

Karla snarled. "Blaming it all on you, I see."

Sandi raised tear drenched eyes to her cousin's. "What do I do now?"

Karla hugged her closer. "You do exactly as you told him. Pick up a few things on Monday, move in with me, and then we'll see about getting you enrolled for the upcoming semester and working toward that degree."

"I don't want to impose, Karls."

Karla snorted. "If it were an imposition, I wouldn't offer." She smiled. "It'll be nice to have you there until you get on your feet."

Sandi rested her head against Karla's shoulder. "I don't know what I'd do without you."

Karla brushed her lips over Sandi's forehead and hugged her again. "You would be just fine without me, but I'm glad I'm here. We'll get through this. Brett Edwards doesn't know what he's up against. When we're done transforming you, he'll either come crawling back on bended knee or suffer the loss the rest of his life."

Sandi chuckled despite the tears that clogged her throat. "Is it wrong for me to want him to come crawling back? I really can't imagine my life without him in it."

"As you stated, he'll always be a part of your life. But *you* need to be a whole person before you can be half a couple. And that's what we're going to work on. I don't know what happened over the years to make you feel so inadequate and unworthy, but we're going to find out and fix that."

For the moment, Sandi believed Karla's vow was possible.

* * *

Brett rubbed his eyes and twiddled with his baseball cap. He cleared his throat and tried to banish the guilt already clouding his decision. True he'd made a mess of things, but the coach's words had rung in his ears all day yesterday and kept him awake most of the night. Maybe it *was* time for him to focus on personal and spiritual growth, and he knew he couldn't do that with his wife and daughter here.

Not if you spend every moment away from home because they are.

Unsure whether the voice was his conscience or that of the Lord, Brett knew truth when he heard it. He made a sandwich, heated a can of soup and then washed his few dishes and put them away.

The next morning, Brett prepared the coffee pot using half the amount of grounds he'd scooped the day before. The brew was still stronger than he liked. He finished off the cup and cut the next one with hot water. *Better,* he thought and added hot water to the remaining coffee in the carafe then placed it back on the hotplate to keep warm. He polished off the remainder of the pot while reading the morning paper.

Since coach honored Sunday as the Lord's Day, there would be no practice, so Brett decided to go to the gym.

He could get in a good workout. He dug around in his dresser for clothes to wear then realized he was once again at a disadvantage.

Everything was dirty, and he had no idea how to operate the washing machine or dryer.

He carried the items into the laundry room where he stood a full minute, mouth hanging open, and glared at the machines.

Small, Large, or Super-size load? Hot/Hot, Cold/Cold, Hot/Cold water temperature? Gentle or Normal cycle?

He dropped the clothes on the floor with a curse, kicked the pile across the room and strode out. The words 'personal growth' mocked his every step. He plopped down into a chair in the living room and pondered his options... Call one of his buddies, call his mother, or call and beg Sandi to come back?

None appealed to him.

"Think, Brett." He tapped the heel of his hand against his temple for emphasis. His phone rang. Joe's number flashed on the screen. Brett answered.

"Hey, Brett, want to meet down at the gym?"

Brett groaned. "Man, I was just thinking the same thing. Need to do up some laundry first, though."

This time Joe groaned. "Laundry is top on my list of crappy jobs."

"Tell me about it."

Joe chortled. "It's funny now, but I'll never forget my first attempt. After my mom died, Dad and I split up the household chores. Laundry was one of mine. I was clueless. Pink underwear just don't cut it in the junior high locker room."

Brett laughed along with his friend.

"So, what did you do then?" He hoped Joe wouldn't guess he was hanging onto the man's every word.

"I asked the Home Ec.' teacher, and she taught me all about sorting the clothes and washing whites in hot, colors in cold. In fact, I still have her hand-written notes in my yearbook." His tone sobered. "That was one tough year, but me and Dad, we pulled through."

Brett's heart went out to his friend. "Never knew that Joe. Sorry for your loss. Hey, let's meet at the gym in a couple of hours."

Joe agreed and they rang off. Brett picked up the clothes he'd kicked into every corner and separated them into two piles. Gaging the size of the loads to be medium, he set the temperature to cold/cold, measured out a capful of detergent according to the directions and threw the color load on to wash. Two hours later he left the house feeling as though he could accomplish anything. He'd managed to wash and dry both loads without turning anything pink or catching the house on fire.

Folding would have to wait though, and there was no way on earth he'd even *attempt* to iron anything. He dropped his work attire at the nearest dry cleaners to be starched and pressed.

* * *

Sandi walked around her and Brett's apartment and

67

double-checked the list of items she'd packed. Emptiness swarmed around her. Engulfed. Overwhelmed. She sat on the bed and cried another bucketload. In the last two days, she'd shed more tears than a body ought to be able to produce. Karla's voice rose in her mind...

Pack your stuff and get out of there before guilt convinces you to stay!

Still, she hesitated and walked through each room filling it with tears and prayers. Exhausted, she lay on her marriage bed. "Oh, God, let no man put asunder what You have joined together. Not even Brett or me. I know I need to do this right now, but I'm asking You, in Jesus' name, to put a hedge of protection around our hearts against anyone or anything that would dare to totally destroy what we've built."

An hour later her cell phone rang and woke her out of a sound sleep.

"Where are you?" Karla demanded. "Candie is getting fussy, and I'm running out of ideas to entertain her."

"I'm sorry. I'll be there as quick as I can." Sandi scrambled from the bed, smoothed the covers, and carried the last few items with her on her way out.

* * *

Two weeks later, Brett floated out of the locker room. Cloud nine was a cliché, and an inadequate one at that. He was soaring through the heavens, looking down on mere mortals.

He'd made the team!

A sharp stab of disappointment pricked his conscience when he spotted Joe walking toward him. He and the man had grown close over the last few months of work, and practice. Though Joe hadn't been cut, he hadn't made the first draft either.

"Congratulations, Brett." Joe extended his hand.

Brett shook the proffered hand. "Thanks, man. Hope you make the second draft."

Joe shrugged. "God willing, but thanks."

Tension buzzed between them. "So…" Brett hesitated.

"Want to have a beer to celebrate?" Joe interjected.

Brett grinned. "I was just about to suggest that but didn't know how you felt about drinking."

Joe laughed. "I believe most things are OK in moderation. Even the Apostle Paul urged Timothy to have a little wine to settle his nerves."

Brett chuckled. "Yeah, and the first miracle Jesus did involved water and wine, and at a celebration."

Two hours later, Brett unlocked the door to his apartment. For the first time in a long time, he wished Sandi were here to share his excitement. A sharp pang of guilt followed that thought. Unexpected grief welled up in his throat. He sank onto the couch and buried his face in his hands.

What am I doing, Lord?

When the Lord remained silent, Brett decided to give Sandi a call.

"Hi, Brett." She answered, and all he heard was

frustration in her tone and Candie's pitiful cries in the background.

"What's the matter with her?"

"What do you care?" Sandi snapped "You haven't called much less seen her in weeks."

"That doesn't mean I don't care. I've been busy."

"Right. Well, I don't have time to discuss it right now. If there's not an emergency, I need to go tend to my daughter." She disconnected the call.

Brett paced the living room. Sandi's words... No, more than her words, her raw emotions bombarded him until his every fiber screeched with tension overlaid by a thick coat of guilt. *What have I done? What am I supposed to do?* Questions swirled in his head like a spinning tornado until they erupted with F5 force. In one sweeping motion he divested the coffee table of its contents.

Next came the bookshelves, which landed on the carpeted floor with a resounding *thud*. Anger spent, he collapsed on the sofa and let the tears come.

* * *

Sandi gathered Candie into her arms and went into the kitchen to retrieve a cold teething ring and mouth gel to rub on the baby's gums. When Candie had settled somewhat, Sandi carried her daughter into the bedroom, sank into the rocking chair and gave into the tears she'd held at bay for hours. Soft sobs shook her entire frame. Not wanting Karla to hear, she turned on the music box which hung on Candie's bed and then buried her face into the blanket cocooning her daughter. When the tears ran out and Candie lay asleep, Sandi rose from the chair and placed the baby in her bed then went into the bathroom to wash her face.

In the weeks since she'd left Brett, her life had taken a turn, many turns, for the better. Until today.

Today she came home from her classes to find Karla in an uproar and Candie an emotional mess. Distraught at the sight of her daughter's runny nose and tear drenched eyes, she'd verbally attacked her cousin. Her heart cringed at the memory of angry words hurled between them. Sandi splashed her face again and left the sanctuary of her bedroom to find Karla and apologize. She found her in the den.

"Hey, Karls."

Karla looked up from her desk and the anguish in her eyes ripped at Sandi's heart. "I'm so sorry to blow up at you the way I did."

Tears filled her cousin's eyes, but she blinked them back and shrugged. "We're bound to have blowups. I'm not used to having a baby around and I'm clueless on how to take care of her when she's sick or upset."

"I know that and should have been more understanding. I so appreciate all you've done and *are* doing for us. I can find a place of my own if you wish."

Anger leapt to life in Karla's midnight eyes. "Did I say I wanted you to do that?"

"No, but..." Her words trailed off at Karla's indignant snort.

"Then don't be stupid."

Sharp pinpricks of emotion stabbed through Sandi. "I am *not* stupid! I'm trying to be considerate. This is your home, your sanctuary, and although I appreciate everything you've done, I'm willing to honor that and get out of your space."

Karla rose, stepped away from the desk. "I invited you here because I love you and want to help you get on your feet. The last thing you need to worry about right now is the responsibility of an apartment, utilities, and all the other stuff that goes along with it. Since you refuse to make Brett help out financially, and the jerk hasn't offered an hour of his time much less a dime of his money, you'd have to get a job along with classes and Candie, and that's just too much for anyone to bear alone. Besides, it's *my* space, and I'll use it as I see fit."

Sandi backed away from the fury and frustration in Karla's tone. "OK. Thank you. I love and appreciate this, Karls, but I have to ask why you're so angry."

"Because you're letting him get away with this bull! Candie is Brett's daughter, too. He should take some responsibility. You've spent the last three years of your life paying for your sin while he goes on and on about his dream, his life, *his* sacrifices. What about you and your sacrifices? What about your dreams? He has no clue what a prize he's got in you, and you refuse to honor yourself enough to stand up and make him see that."

"What do you suggest I do?"

A low growl sounded in Karla's throat. "Ask him for help. Get a lawyer. File for divorce. I don't care what you do, just do *something,* and stop taking it all on yourself as if you somehow deserve to be treated this way."

She turned away and stomped back to plop into her chair behind the desk and picked up a pencil, putting an end to the confrontation. "Now I've got work to do."

Sandi escaped into the bathroom, ran a tubful of water, and added a liberal amount of bubble crystals. The light of truth in Karla's words pierced her heart and shone on so many feelings. Emotions bombarded her—shame, anger, fear, guilt and an awful sense of inadequacy. Voices rose in her mind. *She's right. But I love him. We did it all wrong, we have no right to be happy or fulfilled! It's all my fault, if only I hadn't...*

The litany of her failures went on and on until Sandi had to force down the hot surge of bile in her throat. She swallowed hard, took a mental step back and fought the urge to flee and to escape into the bliss of subconscious acceptance. Unconscious complacency. Years of conditioning rose to the surface. *Don't rock the boat. You made your bed now lie in it. Sometimes your best just isn't good enough...*

The thoughts continued until panic galloped through her veins. Her mind took a quick trip down memory lane, through Karla's and her own childhood. They'd been raised in similar households whose circumstances mirrored each other. Why then had Karla succeeded and she had settled?

A scene emerged in her mind, and all the feelings associated with the incident. Embarrassment, humiliation, and that sickening sensation in the pit of her stomach reminded Sandi of the moment she'd given in to the doubts that had plagued her entire life. A sob rose in her throat. Sandi turned, folded her arms on the side of the tub and wept. When the emotions were spent and the water tepid, she rose from the bath, dried off and dressed in pajamas. A quick check confirmed Candie was fine and sound asleep.

Sandi switched on the baby monitor and took the receiver with her into the den where Karla was still working. "Hey, Karls."

Karla's head snapped up; eyes narrowed. "What's wrong now?"

Sandi blinked at the fresh deluge of tears. "I remembered what happened to make me feel so inadequate and unworthy."

Karla put down her pencil, pushed back from the desk and rose to enfold Sandi in her embrace. "Want to talk about it?"

Sandi considered a moment. "Not really. Not right now anyway. I just don't know what to do to change the way I feel. It's been buried so long. I mean, I thought I'd forgiven and gotten past it, but evidently not."

"Is it something so traumatic you might need counseling?"

Sandi took a deep breath and recalled that moment in time, allowing every gesture and nuance to replay to its fullest. "I believe I can work on it myself. I just don't know where to start. Any suggestions?"

"Tell you what I do to work through every negative thing that happens to me. I pray, meditate, and journal.

Then there's mirror work and affirmations."

Sandi frowned. "Huh?"

Karla kept her arm around Sandi, led her over to the couch, and sat with her. "I've been on this journey of self-discovery for several years now, and these are all tools for intense spiritual and emotional healing. Each has its own unique benefit but when you combine them, the results can be amazing. It's not easy because you have to be brutally honest with yourself and work through all of the negative emotions buried in your mind. But, Sandi, the peace and wholeness you'll gain are well worth the efforts."

Sandi frowned. "Sounds like some kind of new age woo-woo."

Karla laughed. "I guess some would call it that, but what it really is, is a mixture of faith, and psychology. And what's so great is you can do it yourself, and it costs you nothing. Now I'm not saying at some point you won't be better off working with a trained therapist, but this is a great way to open up to the Holy Spirit and embrace the spiritual gifts within you.

Sandi took a deep breath, closed her eyes, and sent a quick prayer heavenward then listened to her heart. "I'm ready."

"Great! OK, the first thing I always do is pray."

Karla took both of Sandi's hands in hers and bowed her head. "Father, we come to you this evening and ask that You look upon our intentions for emotional healing and self-growth. Bless them, Lord Jesus and show us the way. May we seek truth only, because Your Word says that when we know the truth, the truth will set us free.

"Sandi desires to be free from all past emotional, physical, and spiritual traumas. Free from all negative mindsets or half-truths she's been indoctrinated to believe. And, totally free to love, honor and worship You completely and unconditionally in spirit and in truth. She desires to be set free from all guilt and shame associated with those traumas. To accept, receive and offer forgiveness where it is needed. And to emerge with a clear purpose for her life. Your purpose, Lord, not the plans of men. Please bring to light any fears she has and cleanse them away with the awesome power of Your love."

She squeezed Sandi's hands, glanced up. "Is there anything you'd like to add?"

Sandi shook her head.

Karla closed her eyes and bowed her head once more. "Thank You, Lord, for guiding us and for sending Your angels to encamp around us during our sessions. May only those of the highest caliber and deepest love enter into our sacred meetings and may Your Holy Spirit preside over us at all times. We ask this in Jesus' Name. Amen."

"Amen," Sandi chorused and heaved a sigh when a tangible sense of peace and purpose filled the room and enveloped her entire being. "Wow, I've never felt the presence of the Lord so strongly before."

"When you invite God in and ask for His help, and the help of His angels, He, and they, will always show up."

"I'd love to feel this every time I pray."

"God always gives us what we need when we need it. You may not always feel this way every time you pray, but He *is* there, and He lets us feel that consolation when we need it the most."

"So, what do I do?"

Karla rose from the couch, walked over to her desk, opened a drawer, and withdrew a pretty spiral bound book. She prayed over it then brought it back and placed it and a pen in Sandi's hands. "I want you to record everything you think and feel before, during and after our prayer meetings. Write whatever comes to you. Good, bad, it makes no difference. This will give insight to the healing God has for you.

"This is *your* prayer journal. You do not have to tell or show me anything. I won't read it without your permission. But our time with each other and God will bring clarity and inspiration on specific things, messages, and actions you will need to take. The only thing I ask is that you honestly commit to listening and obeying."

"I promise."

Karla nodded then hugged her. "OK your first assignment is to go into a quiet place, put on some soft music if you want, and just sit in God's presence. The sunroom would be perfect, but you can go into my bedroom or the breakfast nook or wherever you feel led. Invite the Holy Spirit into the room or space with you.

"You may feel intense emotions or a change in the atmosphere, don't let that frighten you. For tonight, don't ask any questions or seek guidance. Just open up to the holy Trinity and feel the love God has for you. If you are prompted to write, do so without thinking about, or judging, what you're writing. If not, don't try to force that. It'll come. Leave the baby monitor here."

Sandi handed the monitor to Karla, took the journal and pen, and retired into the tiny room off the kitchen which led into the back yard. A huge, full moon hung like a shining pearl in the velvet sky and filled the room with a soft, luminescent glow. Sandi gazed around in amazement. She'd walked through this room a hundred times in the last few weeks, but never really saw the beauty within the glass-encased walls.

An indoor tropical paradise. The thought popped into her mind and her spirit leapt with joy. Placed in strategic spots to absorb the perfect amount of sunlight to meet each individual need, plants filled the room and perfumed the air. A futon graced one wall, its cushions thick and plush. A bookcase overflowed with literature. Volumes of spiritual tomes spilled over onto shelves, tables, and window ledges. Filled with candles, prayer books, crosses and angels, a tiny table graced one corner, and a huge pillow invited one to sit or kneel before the memorial to God.

Sandi lowered herself onto the soft pad, placed the journal on a corner of the altar, lit a candle and prayed. *Oh, Lord, heavenly Father, I come before You now and open my mind to receive Your instruction, my heart to receive Your grace and my life to receive Your Holy Spirit. Hold me, help me, and guide me. In Jesus' name*

I pray.

She knelt as long as she could and then sat and settled herself to wait until she felt that her meeting with God was over. Before long warmth enveloped the room and words began to form in her mind... *Peace, joy, happiness, wholeness.* Tiny pinpricks of energy surged through her until her entire being hummed with sensation and the words became more than what she heard but something she felt. Something she *experienced.*

Emotion welled in her heart, filled her throat, and poured from her eyes until she lay spent and exhausted but totally steeped in love—saturated, replete, in the deepest, purest, most honest sense of love she'd ever imagined, but never felt. When the intensity lifted, Sandi understood she'd experienced a divine encounter with the lover of her soul. With quiet reverence she rose, blew out the candle and took the journal to her bedroom. She checked on Candie, climbed into the bed, turned on the lamp, opened the book and wrote...

Words can't describe the intensity of what happened so let me just say that tonight I felt, no, experienced, *God's love in a way I never dreamed possible. He became more real to me than ever before and for the first time in my life, I know, truly know, in my heart of hearts and from the depths of my spirit, that I am loved.*

She laid the journal on the bedside table, turned off the light, and descended into the deepest slumber of her life.

* * *

Exhausted and emotionally drained, Brett prayed while cleaning up. His life story played like a movie in his head. Trials and triumphs. Successes and failures. Mistakes and miracles flashed on the screen of his memory until for once in his life, he faced the truth about himself and his selfish nature.

Acceptance was a hard pill to swallow, but he forced it down with a dose of humility and a prayer for forgiveness and guidance.

God help me. He picked up his phone and hit the button to dial Sandi's number. After a couple of rings, the call went straight to voicemail. He hung up without leaving a message then scrolled through his contact list until he found Karla's number. He hesitated, then hit the call button.

"Hello."

She sounded anything but friendly or welcoming.

"Hey, Karla, it's Brett."

"I know who it is. What do you want?"

The ice in her voice pierced his conscience. "I tried to reach Sandi but couldn't. Is she around?"

"She's sleeping. I imagine after the day she had, she shut the phone off so both she and Candie could get a decent night's rest."

"Oh." Brett closed his eyes, pinched the bridge of his nose and swallowed pride and fear. "I'm sorry."

"I'm not the one you should apologize to."

"Yes you are, and I am. I'll apologize to Sandi, too."

"Well at least it's a start."

His heart lightened at the grudging respect in her voice.

"Thanks for all you're doing for them, Karls. I realized tonight I have a lot of work to do, and it'll probably take some time to figure out what's next, but I want you to know I honestly do appreciate you."

A heavy sigh came across the phone. "I think Sandi realized the same thing tonight. I'll tell you like I told her: You need to be a whole person before you can be half a couple."

"I know. Pray for me will you?"

At her assurance she would, Brett hung up. He called Sandi's number again, left an apology and requested she call him at her earliest convenience. He then took a shower, crawled into bed, and prayed for God to show him his next step.

It took three days for Brett's phone to ring. Sandi's name flashed on the screen. He rolled away from his desk and walked to the office window overlooking the city park. "Hey there."

"I'm sorry."

The stiffness in her voice belied the words but Brett chose to let it pass.

"Me too. How's Candie doing?"

"She's teething. Pretty miserable."

"Anything I can do?"

"As a matter of fact, there is." Her voice had hardened a degree.

His heart lurched then set off at a gallop.

"You can come visit or take her for the weekend or something. I could use a break, and I'm sure she misses you. You could also help out financially. I'm back in school and Karla's been gracious enough to refuse what little I can offer, but that's not fair to her and there's no way I can work, take care of Candie, *and* go to school."

"How much do you need?"

A snort preceded her words. "Brett, I'm sure anything will help."

"You still have your bank card, right?"

"Of course."

"Well use what you need to."

"I'd rather use what you allow. Don't ever want it said I've overspent or taken advantage of you."

This time Brett literally cringed, but he bit back on the anger and frustration at the venom in her voice. "Should I mail you a check?"

"That or you can bring it when you come to pick Candie up."

He cleared his throat and prepared for her reaction to his next words. "That's just it, Sandi, I'm not sure when that'll be. I made the team. We practice every evening and on weekends. Except for Sunday. Season starts in less than a month."

"Just send a check, then." She hung up before he could say another word.

* * *

Sandi ground her teeth and swallowed the emotions clogging her airways. *He made the team. His mistress had won.* She burst into tears. She folded her arms on the kitchen table, buried her face in them and let the emotions storm through.

Spent, and oddly calm afterward, she got up and splashed cold water on her face and then patted it dry with a paper towel, glad Karla was out at the moment. At least she wouldn't have to face her cousin's anger along with the torrent of feelings roiling in her own heart.

Sandi ripped another paper towel off the roll and carried it with her to check on Candie who was fast asleep in her crib. Picking up her journal, she carried it and the baby monitor with her into the sunroom. She settled herself on the cushion in front of the altar, lit a candle and prayed.

Help me, oh Lord, to know what to do.

She sat still until words started to flow in her journal. Pain, anger, and frustration poured forth, filling the pages until peace and clarity shone through. Although she was unsure as to how much she should support Brett in his dream, she would let him live it.

She wouldn't, however, be his groupie. She would continue working towards her degree which would enable her to support herself and her daughter should the need arise. And somehow, some way, she'd repay her cousin for all Karla had done for them. Not monetarily, of course, as Karla would never accept that, but somehow Sandi would not let her generosity be in vain.

Two days later she received a nice fat check from

Brett. Sandi opened a checking account and used the funds to replenish Candie's and her own personal needs. Then she splurged and took Karla out for dinner while the baby stayed with her parents.

Karla ordered each of them a glass of wine then raised hers in a toast. "I'm so proud of you."

Sandi touched her glass to Karla's. "And I'm so grateful to you. I couldn't have done any of this without your support and guidance. Even my parents don't understand, much less support my decisions the way you do."

Karla's smile was rich with compassion. A hint of laughter lit her midnight gaze. "Our parents are old school. Nothing is wrong with that, but life is progressive. Always moving. Always evolving. Always expanding. And if we stay stuck in our ways of doing things, and ways of thinking and don't evolve with it, we'll never live up to our potential.

"The key is to allow people to be who they are. Let them travel their own journey and realize that, although their ways may influence us, they don't have to control us. We're all here, on this planet, in this realm to do specific things for God and our fellow man. Even for our planet. But realizing that and choosing to live and walk in it is up to each individual person. Our job is not to judge or criticize, only to love and to guide."

Sandi nodded. "You know, I've always felt there was so much more depth to life and spirituality than I learned growing up, but never in my wildest dreams would have imagined the closeness I could feel to God."

Karla acknowledged her words with a slight nod then spoke. "Faith is an internal compass on our path to God. Whatever tools we use to sharpen and grow our faith, again are as personal and unique as the individuals incorporating them into their worship practice. The thing is personal, and spiritual growth is an ongoing process. Sure, there are times of rest and recovery, but we should not get complacent but strive to reach that next level until we recognize God's hand in all things."

The waiter brought their food. Sandi contemplated her meal for a few minutes then smiled at her cousin. "I'd like to do what you do, Karls. I'd love to help others discover their truth, explore their depths, and strive for their highest potential with God."

Karla's pleasure was palatable. "Well, there's no shortage of need for more life or spiritual coaches. Concentrate on getting your life in order, get your degree, and then I say go for it."

Sandi hesitated, took a sip followed by a bite of food, and then put a voice to the feelings swirling inside. "I wonder if I even want this particular degree. In fact, I'm seriously considering changing it or dropping school altogether."

Karla's eyes widened.

"Only this particular school, Karls, not my education. I just don't know what to go into, but I'd like to be in the counseling and perhaps ministerial field."

Karla too, took a few minutes to contemplate her meal before answering. "Then I suggest you spend a lot of time in prayer and ask God what He wants you to do and ask for help and guidance to move in that direction. Think about it, Sandi. What's your passion? What brings you the most joy?"

Sandi took another drink then put the glass down. "I've always loved graphic design and art in general, but since my last conversation with Brett and the revelation that occurred while praying and journaling, I've been rethinking my life plan."

Karla arched her brow in question. "Would you care to expound on that revelation? Remember, as your coach, you don't have to tell me anything, but as your cousin I'd like to know how you're doing. Really, deep down honest, doing."

Sandi smiled. "We've shared our lives forever, Karls and I'm really, deep down honestly doing OK. As for the revelation, I realized I deserve to be treated with equal respect as my husband. Not that he ever dishonored or disrespected me in the way that some people do. You know, abuse and all that. But my dreams, my desires are just as important as his. And that wholeness you talked about, wholeness of heart, of spirit, I've never really felt that, and I want to now."

"Attaining wholeness can be a lifelong process."

"I understand that. I also realized that once Brett and I married, I put all of his needs, his dreams, and *his* plans ahead of my most basic need, the need for self-expression. I didn't give a voice to my soul or even what I wanted in any aspect. Not in love, not in marriage, not in equality on any level. It was all about Brett. Then, after Candie came along, I got shoved even farther down the list."

"That happens with a lot of women, Sandi. You'd be amazed at how many. We have a God-given nature to nurture—even women who work outside the home—but for women who choose to stay at home, there's greater risk of losing yourself. Society has shifted from holding 'caretaker' up as an honorable choice. It's so easy to go to work, put kids in daycare or elderly parents in a facility, and so women who choose to stay home are now fighting a stigma that society has placed on that choice. It puts added stress on your emotions. And that stress creates a see-saw effect.

"For a while you do all you can to put your husband and kids first because that's what you're supposed to do—all the while, in the back of your mind, seeds of resentment can grow because society says you're crazy for living the way you're living. Then, you start to feel as if you don't matter, because you're not 'living up to your potential' or accomplishing anything important, because, after all, taking care of your family isn't as important as taking care of yourself."

Karla sipped her drink, took another bite of her dinner then continued. "And, in a way, that's true. We do have to nurture ourselves—especially our spiritual selves, because how can we love our neighbor as ourselves if we don't love ourselves? But again, we have to find a balance. There are roles for husbands and wives laid out in the Bible, and when lived out properly by both spouses, marriage is actually beautiful. No one gets lost, because each spouse is fulfilling the needs of the other the way it's supposed to be.

"The problem in your marriage, Sandi, isn't that you did anything wrong by seeing to the needs of your husband and daughter. The problem was that Brett wasn't loving you the way Christ loves the church."

Karla paused, and the silence hovering over the table made Sandi's heart beat a little faster. She knew that silent pose. Karla was getting ready to say something crucial. Sandi mentally braced for what was coming.

"You have some culpability in that, Sandi, because you should've talked to Brett about it. Told him how you felt, maybe took a course or counseling that taught you guys how to live out your Biblical roles. But ultimately, you couldn't force Brett to hold up his end.

"And that's where nurturing yourself also comes in. We are to look after our spouses, but we can't rely on any other human being to make us happy. Only God can accomplish that, so we have to put our spiritual health first. If you take care of your spiritual health, everything else, including your hopes and dreams, will fall into place—even if your spouse is a self-centered jerk who puts sports above his own wife."

Sandi laughed lightly at Karla's bluntness. She nodded. "And that's exactly what I haven't done. But no more. And I'd love to help others do the same, to find balance between what they feel they *have* to do and what they want to do with their life."

"Have you considered what changes you'd have to make in your curriculum to achieve that end?"

Sandi shrugged. "Not really. I've had a lot of different

thoughts and ideas, but none of them seem to be substantial or make any sense when it comes down to it."

Listening to the whispers in her heart, she continued. "I've always loved fitness and nutrition but have no desire to work in a clinical or hospital environment even though that's where the money really is. And now..."

"Now what?"

Tiny bubbles of heat burst beneath her skin and fear rose to strangle her words as a new dream emerged in her heart. Sandi squashed it with a shake of her head. "A silly pipe dream."

"I've found that what most people deem a silly pipe dream turns out to be their soul's calling."

Sandi choked down the insecurity with more wine, looked her cousin in the eye and confided in the one person she knew would never judge or try to talk her out of her innermost desires. "All this journaling has brought back the dream of writing."

A smile lit up Karla's entire face. "Yes," she said with an emphatic pump of her fist. "You've always been great at stringing words together for maximum impact. I think it's a wonderful dream!"

"But how am I going to support myself and Candie by writing if things don't work out between Brett and me?"

"By not limiting yourself. You are a terrific artist, you love fitness and nutrition, you were the best cheerleader so you're great at encouraging people, and you write like a seasoned professional. Talk to your guidance counselor at school. Maybe branch off into journalism or psychology or kinesiology but add in some creative writing courses.

"Or, better yet, change to a BFA or MFA for that matter, with emphasis on writing. There are so many options... editor, copy editor, copywriter, teacher... and, with your artistic ability, the opportunities are endless."

"You really think so?"

Karla nodded.

"But what if things *do* work out with my marriage. How would I put it all together then and still be able to take proper care of my husband, household, and daughter. I'd love to have more children too."

"It'll work out because you'll keep studying and growing and there's always the option of working from home."

Sandi blinked back tears at Karla's sheer faith in her and raised her glass in salute. "Talk about a great cheerleader."

Karla clinked glasses with Sandi and smiled.

* * *

Brett waved in response to Joe's goodbye and then bent to tie his shoes. He straightened, slung his gym bag over his shoulder and walked out of the locker room. The emptiness he'd felt in the last few weeks hadn't lessened as the season opener approached, as he'd hoped. In fact, the idea of playing, of winning a game with no one there to support him, to cheer him on, was pretty grim indeed.

His cell phone rang. Brett looked at the name that flashed across the screen. He grimaced then answered. "Hi, Dad."

"Hey, Brett, haven't heard from you or Sandi in a while. How's everything and how's my beautiful granddaughter?"

Brett cringed and cleared his throat. "Uh... well, Dad, I'm doing fine. Made the team..."

His words trailed off at his father's triumphant yelp.

"That's wonderful! When does season start? Perhaps Mom and I can come down and watch you play. Or better yet, park the RV somewhere nearby and stay for the season. Maybe follow the team."

He wouldn't have to be alone after all. The excitement he tried to muster up failed Brett. "That would be nice, Dad."

"Your enthusiasm overwhelms me."

Brett sighed and rubbed his eyes. *Time for truth.* He took a deep breath and informed his father of the current state of his marriage.

"Aw, son, wish you'd have called us earlier. You know we would've been there in a heartbeat to help in any way we can."

Instead of the guilt and chastisement he expected, his father's words warmed Brett's heart. "That's just it, Dad, half the time I have no idea what I'm doing, much less what anyone else can do to help."

"You still love her?"

"Of course, I love her. I just don't know what to do now that I've made a mess of things."

"Talking's always a good start."

"True, but I have no idea where to begin. I've always wanted to play pro football. With that not possible, I thought NPIFL would fill the void."

"Has it?"

Brett shook his head, the movement emphasizing the words that poured out of his mouth. "No, and I don't know where to go from here. I've made the team, and I'm going to play. Might be my only chance, and I owe it to myself and that dream, the dream you and mom wanted and supported as long as I can remember, to at least play this one season. Besides, y'all always taught me to finish what I started no matter what."

"Yes we did, son, but not at the expense of your happiness and definitely not at the expense of your marriage and family. May I make a suggestion?"

"Sure."

"Although we raised you in faith, we never pushed you in any direction when it came to developing your walk with God. Figured you needed to take responsibility for that and grow your relationship with Him in your own way, own time. But I can tell you this much, no guidance is as complete as His.

"Find a church, Bible study, or support group of some sort, and see if you can get to the root of your feelings. Sort 'em out, get clear about what you want, what you need and expect, then talk to your wife. Don't just talk to her, but listen, really listen to Sandi. Find out what she wants, needs and expects, then and only then, make some decisions. There's nothing that can't be resolved with honesty, compassion, and commitment."

"Hey Brett!"

Brett's head jerked up. His eyes met the coach's.

Coach mimed an apology for interrupting Brett's call.

Brett nodded and held up a finger to indicate he'd be off in a minute, then returned his attention to his father.

"Thanks, Dad. I'll do that. And it would be wonderful if you and Mom can come down for our opening game and follow the team." They shared a couple more pleasantries then ended their call.

Brett tucked his phone into the pocket of his jeans and shook hands with his coach.

"How's it going?"

"Great, just got off the phone with my dad. He and Mom want to come and follow the team."

"Wonderful! Where are they from?"

"Sherman."

"That's not too far. It'll be nice to meet them. How're things going with the wife?"

Brett shrugged. "She's back in school. I sent her a check the other day but other than that, nothing's changed."

"How's the baby?"

"Teething."

Coach murmured sympathy for Candie's discomfort then asked where Brett was headed.

He shrugged. "Home I guess. Got a set of blueprints due in a couple of days, reckon I'll work on them a while then hit the sack early."

Coach slapped him on the shoulder. "Sounds good. I like to see my players avoiding the temptation to drink and party. In fact, I'm thinking about starting a Bible study for those interested. You game?"

Can't make it any clearer than that, can you God? "Sure, text me the deets and I'll be there."

Coach's pleasure at Brett's answer was obvious in the way he smiled and shook hands again before continuing on to his own car.

Brett climbed into his truck, surprised, and awed at how God had shown Himself so clearly that afternoon.

* * *

Sandi's heart curled into a tiny wad of fear when her phone vibrated, and her father-in-law's name flashed on the screen. Before she could decide whether to answer, her guidance counselor walked out of the office and summoned her. Sandi pressed the button to send the call to voicemail, stood, and followed the lady into her office.

Two hours later, she rushed home, excitement replacing every other emotion in her sphere. The counselor had listened, more than listened, she'd *understood*, Sandi's need for expression and love of the written word. Together they'd outlined a plan to change Sandi's degree program to a Bachelor's of Fine Arts with emphasis on writing.

She'd suggested Sandi continue with her art and graphics design classes and recommended a couple of electives in Theology and Religious Science. She had even gone so far as to research websites, journals and periodicals through which Sandi could begin writing for both name recognition and income.

She couldn't wait to tell Karla!

She'd barely pulled into the drive when Brett's father called again, and Sandi realized she'd forgotten to listen to his earlier voice mail. "Hello, Jack."

"Hi, Sandi gal! How's that beautiful granddaughter of mine?"

"She's teething so a bit uncomfortable, but other than that Candie's fine. How are you and Martha?"

"We're doing great. Listen, sweetie, Brett told us y'all are having a bit of a spat. Not going to pry, but Martha and I want you to know we're here for you, and if you need anything at all, be sure and call. Y'hear?"

Sandi thanked him and hung up, then ran into the house to hug her daughter and share her news with Karla.

* * *

Brett sat with five of his teammates at Coach's house for the second week in a row as the group continued to study First Corinthians. As they embarked on chapter thirteen, he began to see how much he'd lacked in showing Sandi true love. The deeper they delved into the scriptures on love, the more convicted he felt. Convicted and convinced his father had been right. He needed to get to the root of his feelings, sort them out and then have a heart to heart conversation with his wife.

* * *

Sandi read 1 Corinthians 13 for the hundredth time, maybe thousandth. *Love bears all things, believes all things, hopes all things, and endures all things. Love never fails.*

She loved that Scripture. It's what had kept her hanging on through her rocky marriage to Brett. Those words gave her hope and kept her faith alive during the roughest patches of learning to be a wife and mother. Through it all she hung on, believing *'What God has joined together let no man put asunder.'*

But this time, instead of hope, Sandi felt an overwhelming depression settle in her heart. She still had no idea where her marriage was headed. Although she kept up with Brett's football team via the newspaper, radio, and Internet, she had yet to attend a game. She'd stuck to her vow to let Brett live his dream while she pursued hers.

Still, she wondered and worried, and, in the deepest part of her heart and soul, she missed him. Terribly. So what if they'd done it all wrong? They got pregnant before the wedding and had a baby instead of honeymoon. Those weren't reasons enough for the marriage not to work. But it hadn't. They'd sinned, and the wages of sin was death. In this case the possible death of their marriage.

No! I won't believe that! Her heart cried out in denial. *Jesus overcame death on Calvary.* She'd asked

His forgiveness for her sin of the flesh long ago, and she knew without a doubt that her pre-marital choices would not condemn her marriage. Jesus had washed away those sins.

Sandi firmly believed in His resurrection and hoped for the resurrection of her marriage. Biting back tears of frustration, she read the scripture again and prayed.

God, please show me what to do, how to work this out. But more than that, Father, please show me how to pull myself out of this pit of despair.

"I put before you life and death, therefore choose life."

The words echoed in her heart on the heels of that still, small Voice in her soul and Sandi knew what she had to do. She had to make a choice. The choice to move on or wallow in depression and self-pity for the rest of her life. She had to decide and accept joy over despair, peace over anger, love over bitterness and hate. She had to *choose* to climb out of the pit of death and celebrate life.

Looking around she realized Easter was fast approaching and neither she nor Karla had even talked about decorating. Putting her Bible aside, she sought Karla and asked about decorations for the upcoming holiday.

Karla shrugged. "I've never decorated for any holiday except Christmas, but if you want to run to the store and pick some up, I'll keep an eye on Candie."

Grateful for the reprieve from her thoughts, Sandi vowed not to worry over what looked like an incredible lack of progress in the situation and did her best not to dwell on the possibility of an answer she didn't want to hear.

* * *

Brett drove by Karla's apartment complex. Heart pounding, he realized how much he missed his wife and daughter. He missed Sandi's gentle strength, her kindness and generous heart, and he missed his daughter's crooked smile and little girl giggles. He'd done some serious soul searching in the past couple of weeks. That, along with counseling sessions with his coach and parents, he understood the magnificence of his errors and wondered if Sandi would ever forgive him much less consider reconciliation.

He knew there was only one way to find out, but pride and fear kept him lodged within the confines of the vehicle. He began to pray, *really* pray, repenting and surrendering and pleading with God for a second chance.

A movement at the corner of his eye caught his attention. Brett watched as a car like Sandi's made a pass through the parking lot and then pulled into a vacant spot two rows up on the right. His heart lurched when he saw her disembark with two shopping bags in each hand.

Now's your chance!

Without stopping to second-guess himself, he picked up the spray of Easter lilies he'd brought in case he got up the nerve to approach her and opened his car door while calling her name.

She turned, and an assortment of emotions flitted across her features. The door opened behind her, and Karla stepped out.

"Everything all right out here?"

"I'd like to talk to Sandi, if it's OK with her."

Sandi eyed the flowers in his hand then gave Karla the bags and murmured something to her. Karla acknowledged the words with a nod, took the packages, and went back inside.

Brett held the bouquet toward her. "I know these are your favorites. Hope you don't mind that I picked them up."

She buried her nose in the fragrant blooms then raised her gaze to his once more. "What are you doing here, Brett? I haven't seen or heard from you in weeks."

"I'd hoped we could go to church together Sunday."

"I thought your games were Friday, Saturday and Sunday."

"They normally are, just not on Easter Sunday. I know we haven't gone to church much through the years of our marriage, but I've been attending a Bible study with the coach and some of the team members. I figured this was a good time to start going again. I'd like to take you and Candie with me then maybe out to lunch so we can talk. Karla is welcome to come along if you and she want it that way."

"I'm sorry, Brett, but we've already made plans with our families to have lunch and an Easter egg hunt for the little ones. You're welcome to join us though."

Brett bit back his disappointment. The last thing he

wanted was a family outing when he hadn't been part of the familial unit for months. "How about an early breakfast, then church? I promise to get you back in plenty of time for the festivities you've planned. I'd really like to talk to you, Sandi, to apologize for the way I've treated you and to see if there's a chance of you coming home."

He reached for her, and she stiffened. Hope and despair collided on her face, churned into anger. Color exploded in her cheeks. She jerked away. "You think it's that easy, Brett? Just bring a bunch of flowers and sweet talk your way back into our good graces after all this time? You've a lot of nerve thinking that."

"I don't think that at all, Sandi. Easter's a time of resurrection, reconciliation, and restoration. I'd hoped we could at least start to work out our differences, most of which, I know are my fault. Have you hardened your heart so much that I don't even stand a chance?"

Her sigh spoke volumes. Tears rushed to her eyes and tore at his heart.

"I'll have breakfast and go to church with you, Brett, and we'll talk. But it'll take more than one discussion to resolve our differences."

He touched her cheek, thrilled when she didn't pull away this time. "I agree, but the way I see it, one conversation is a step in the right direction. Shall I pick y'all up or do you want to meet me?"

"Text me the time and place and we'll meet you."

"Thank you," he whispered then turned and walked back to his car.

* * *

Sandi gazed at the star-studded sky at four-thirty Sunday morning. Her conversation with Brett and subsequent chat with Karla the evening before had rolled around in her brain all night, making for a restless slumber. The way he looked, all healthy and athletic, those moss green eyes pleading and sincere, and his thick auburn hair mussed as though he'd raked his hands through it as he always did when tired or upset, had her lifelong dream of being a wife and mother reasserting itself in her mind.

Clashing with the new goals she'd set for herself.

She turned away from the window, checked on her daughter, and then picked up her journal and the baby monitor and tiptoed into the sunroom. After lighting the candles, she knelt to pray then sat to wait on the Holy Spirit for guidance and direction. Words of wisdom, peace and love flowed into her heart, and she recorded them onto the pages of her journal. She stayed in prayer long moments after the messages stopped, assured of what she had to do.

She had to stay strong and remain true to herself. She had to honor her plans and dreams and place as high of value on them as she did her husband's and daughter's. With this resolution in mind, she showered and dressed and had Candie ready to meet Brett when his text message came through.

* * *

Brett met Sandi when she pulled into the parking lot and opened the door so she could step out of the car. The light gray skirt and blazer with lavender blouse and bold print scarf brought out the smoke in her eyes and clung to her shapely form in a way he hadn't paid attention to in quite some time. Her luscious wheat colored hair fell in soft waves across her shoulders and back. He shut her door then opened the back passenger one so she could get Candie out of the car seat. The moment his daughter laid eyes on him she shrieked with pleasure and struggled while her mother tried to unfasten the straps across her shoulders and legs.

Brett placed a hand on Sandi's back. "Let me get her."

Sandi moved out of the way and let him gather Candie up in his arms. Her childish gibberish filled him with a mixture of joy and guilt. The family made their way into the restaurant and waited to be seated.

Once settled, he reached for Sandi's hand. "Thank you for agreeing to this."

"Thank you for inviting us. I won't pretend I'm not surprised considering the lack of communication between us."

Before he could say more, a waiter appeared to take their drink orders. Each took a few moments to peruse the menus and knew what they wanted to eat when he returned. That taken care of, Brett once again reached for Sandi's hand.

"I know I've been a jerk for a long time Sandi, and I'm sorry. I've been so disappointed in the way my life turned out that I turned a blind eye to the blessings. That's no excuse, I know, but the truth, nonetheless. I've missed you and Candie. I didn't realize how much until lately, and I'd really like for the chance to be the kind of husband you deserve and father she needs."

"That's all fine, good, and well, Brett, but like I said last night, it's going to take more than one conversation for us to work out our differences. I've done a lot of soul searching and growth and I can't, correction, I *won't* go back to being a silent partner in a one sided relationship. I deserve more from you and from myself."

"I understand and agree. Let's just take it one day, one step at a time."

Their meals arrived and put an end to further conversation as each concentrated on eating while they took turns making sure Candie ate more food than she wore. When the plates were empty and stomachs appeased, Sandi requested a refill of her coffee. She smiled her thanks when the waiter poured a fresh cup and then returned her attention to Brett.

"The Mudbugs seem to be doing well for their first season."

He looked surprised. "I didn't know you were keeping up with the team."

She shrugged. "I catch the scores on TV."

"If you ever want to attend a game, I can make sure you have tickets at the box stand."

"Thanks, I'll keep that in mind." Sandi glanced at her

watch. "We'd better get a move on if we don't want to be late for church."

They gathered their things and left the restaurant.

After church services were over, Sandi reiterated her invitation for Brett to join the family lunch and Easter egg hunt. Not wanting to intrude but desiring more time with them, he agreed but vowed to himself he'd leave at the first indication of anyone's discomfort.

* * *

Three months later

Karla tipped her glass against Sandi's in a toast. "Words seem inadequate at expressing how proud of you I am."

Sandi sipped the cool, white liquid then smiled over the rim of her glass at her cousin. "Nor are they adequate to show my love and appreciation for all you've done for me. You've supported me in more ways than one and I'll be forever grateful."

"I'm just glad to see you sticking to the program and continuing to work on your path of healing and growth. I wasn't sure with Brett back in the picture you would."

Sandi sipped her wine in silence, her mind wandering back over the time since she and Brett met for breakfast Easter morning. "There's been a lot of changes in a few short months, hasn't there?"

Karla nodded. "I'm really surprised and pleased. I never thought Brett would step up to plate. I'm glad I was wrong."

Sandi cocked her eyebrow and waited for Karla to elaborate. Her cousin shrugged, obviously disconcerted with Sandi's scrutiny.

"I've worked with a lot of people and, well, most men who put sports before their wives and children end up divorced. I was all ready and prepared to help you through that, but now it looks like I won't have to."

"We're not back together completely yet."

"Yeah, but he's been the model husband and father for months now. Calling nearly every day. Sending financial support. Picking Candie up at least once a week after work to spend the evening with her and allowing you time to yourself or for us to have time together. Like now. I hope it's a permanent change for him and not just a temporary thing to get y'all back."

Sandi sighed. "So, do I. He hasn't pressured me to come home at all, seems content with the situation as it is for now. We've had some really productive conversations lately and he seems to understand that when, *if* I return, there will be ground rules. I refuse to go back into the same dysfunctional relationship I walked out of."

"That's good to hear, Sandi. Just remember, emotional/spiritual healing and growth are lifelong processes. You've done some really amazing internal work, and I'd hate to see you backslide. Although that's normal too. Being prepared for when it happens is the key to overcoming."

"Guess we'll see for sure what his true motives are once football season is over. Who would've thought the

Mudbugs would go into playoffs their very first season?"

"Does he plan to play again next year?"

Sandi shrugged. "I don't know. We haven't talked that far ahead. I'll graduate in December, which is a miracle in itself. Changing my focus and curriculum turned out to be the best decision I could have made."

Karla raised her glass again. "Yeah, and your writing has taken on a whole new level of depth and meaning. Thank you, again, for suggesting we collaborate on a book. I'd have never ventured to write one on my own."

Pleasure shivered through her. Excitement rose in bumps on her skin. Sandi leaned forward in her chair to touch her glass against Karla's with a grin and a wink. "Maybe that's something *you* should work on."

Karla laughed.

"Can you believe how quick and easy it was to find an agent and publisher for this book considering neither of us have written anything of that magnitude before?"

Karla raised her glass in salute. "Hey, your blog is what caught their attention."

"I know, but seriously? Have you *ever* heard of anything like this happening so fast?"

Karla shook her head.

"I'm forever amazed at how God works and how perfectly all things come together when left in His hands."

"Never lose that awe and reverence, Sandi, and God will take you places and accomplish things through you that you never dreamed possible."

* * *

Brett Edwards knelt in a pew on the eve of Good Friday, awed and humbled at the grace of God and the many blessings which continued to pour into his life, even a year after he'd caused his wife to leave. After the Louisiana Mudbugs culminated their maiden season with a championship, he'd continued to meet with the coach and team members for Bible study and fellowship. He'd stayed the course in reconciling the mistakes of his past and in becoming the kind of man he, his wife, his parents and his Father could be proud of.

Sandi finished school in December with a BFA and a book contract. She would enroll in grad school for her Masters in the fall after a much needed and well deserved break during the spring and summer semesters. *Break* was relative in term only, as she would be tied up in edits and revisions most of that time.

He glanced at the diamond ring tied into the bow of the bouquet of lilies that lay on the seat next to him and hoped this Easter would be a new beginning for them as a family. He heard the church door open and glanced over his shoulder to see her enter. Rising, he picked up the flowers and met her midway down the aisle where a plethora of stars shone through the skylight. Taking her hand, he dropped to one knee and watched surprise and pleasure light her eyes, brighter than a thousand stars when she spotted the ring.

"Will you do me the honor of coming home as my wife? I promise to love, honor, cherish and treasure you in ways previously unimaginable."

Without a word, Sandi untied the bow, gave him the ring and held her breath while he slipped the diamond she'd longed for flush against the wedding band on her finger.

The End

Dear Reader,

Like Brett, how often do we let poor decisions of the past control and shape our future instead of forgiving, letting go and moving forward into the great plan God has for our lives?

I know I've done so. Many times. But, like Brett and Sandi, I work with God on a continual basis to release, trust, and be healed of old mindsets and beliefs which hinder Him and/or block His movement in my circumstances.

Like Karla, I believe life is progressive. Always moving. Always evolving. Always expanding. And if we stay stuck in our ways of doing things, or ways of thinking and don't evolve with it, we'll never live up to our potential.

I've mentioned things in this story you may not be aware of... Journaling, affirmations, mirror work. Perhaps you've heard of them but were unsure of their value. I've personally used these modalities in my quest to know God (my Lord, Father, Savior, Brother, Advocate and Friend personified) on a more intimate level as well as for mental/emotional healing and spiritual/self-growth.

It's been said that when the student is ready, the teacher will appear. May these thoughts, ideas and words expressed throughout this story be a source of inspiration, healing, and teaching for YOU!

As always, if you don't know Him, I pray that you seek a personal relationship with Jesus. If you do, I urge you to pursue a closer, more intimate walk with Him.

And, as always, THANK YOU for your continued support of my writing – may you find joy in reading.

Cathy's Angel

Cathy Johnson headed out the back door of her modest home. The sun peeked over the horizon, turning the sky various shades of pink and gold. Fingers of orange and yellow reached down, bathing the path she jogged with light. Flowers blooming along the roadside and in fields across the way perfumed the spring air. Her heart swelled with gratitude, and she communed with God in her heart and aloud.

"Thank You, Lord, for this beautiful morning and all the blessings in my life. I worship and adore You, Jesus, and I surrender this day to You. Give me Your will and Your strength to get through the challenges I may face."

Taking a deep breath, she rounded the curve and picked up her pace a notch. "I give You my successes—which are all Yours anyway—and my failures, which are all mine, and ask only for Your strength, wisdom, and direction. Oh, and a little help in the physical realm would be nice. I'm so grateful that Your Spirit infuses me with the strength and energy I need to handle my day, but Lord a flesh-and-bone helping hand now and again would be great! And it doesn't have to be a man, either."

She snorted. The men she'd met since her husband's death had all but run off in a panic when they met her children. A shadowy figure came into view, interrupting her prayer.

"What's he doing on my road?" she demanded, her heart switching from gratitude to attitude in the span of a thought. "This is my road, my time, the only hour of the day I have all to myself, free from the rat race of my life and I don't like sharing it." She glared at the unwelcome stranger when he ran by with a nod and smile.

* * *

Jared rolled his eyes with a grunt.

"Lord, the worst sight in the world this time of day is a frowning woman," he muttered under his breath, as he jogged past the petite, green-eyed, brunette who looked as though she'd swallowed a lemon. Shaking the image from his mind, he forced his thoughts back to more pleasant ones. That, coupled with running, was the only way he could prepare for his daily obligations.

Being a self-employed Computer Programmer & Networker had it's pro's and con's, more often leading to the con's. Day after day of setting up businesses, networking them into or out of the Information Super Highway and training their employees didn't just put a strain on his mind, but emotions, as well. Relief could be found in an early morning run, which was why he leased a house on this particular road in this specific subdivision last week. Never one for idleness, the month-long hiatus from work that he'd allowed himself was currently filled with unpacking and settling into his new home.

Rounding the final curve in the road, which would take him back to the house, he saw his unknown running partner sitting on the ground and holding her foot.

* * *

"Great, Lord, just great. All I need today, *any* day, is a sprained ankle. Besides, I asked for a well-trained angel *not* a sprained ankle," she bemoaned, as though God had actually misunderstood her one consistent plea. Being the single mother of four, ages three to eleven, and running a small home-based business was hectic to say the least. Her only salvation had been the peace and quiet she found in an early morning run. Burying her head against her knee, Cathy loosened her tennis shoe and fought the urge to sob. Still, the tears came, rolling slowly down her cheeks. "I'm sorry, Lord."

Nothing induced repentance quicker than a crisis. "What am I going to do now?"

Hearing footsteps, she looked up to see the man she'd passed earlier fast approaching. He paused in front of her.

"Are you all right?" He kept jogging in place to bring his heart rate down and cool his muscles.

Cathy ignored the shivers of delight that curled up her spine at the sound of his velvety-rough voice and glared at him for the second time that day. Nice voice, dumb question. Unless he was blind, he could see the tears on her face. She swiped at them and dropped the blame squarely at his feet. "No, I'm not all right. I twisted my ankle and it's all your fault."

He halted his movements. "Me? What'd I do? I don't even know you, Lady."

"You interrupted my quiet time."

"Well excuse me for living and breathing." He glared at her. The gold flames of fury sparking his dark eyes demanded that she not interrupt his tirade. Still, she jerked up her chin a notch, and narrowed her gaze, but bit her tongue.

"I happen to be new to this neighborhood and haven't run across any signs informing me to 'stay out of Ms. ... What's your name?"

"Cathy."

"Ms. Cathy's quiet time."

To Jared's surprise and consternation, she burst into tears.

"I – I'm s-sorry. I-I'm u-usually not s-so rude."

"Of course, you're not. PMS I'm sure." He patted her shoulder, feeling even more awkward. Women were never his strong point. They were too emotional, and his analytical mind couldn't cope.

"I d-don't h-have time for PMS."

Her wail confirmed his opinion.

"M-my oldest c-child is f-fixing breakfast for the o-other -t-three, and I've g-got t-to g-get home."

OK Lord, Jared thought with a sigh. You leave me no choice but to play Good Samaritan. Reaching down, he swung her up in his arms.

She stiffened.

"Easy now, I'm not going to hurt you. Where do you live?"

"T-two blocks down, f-first house on the r-right." Unable to resist the comfort his broad shoulder offered, Cathy buried her head in it and sniffled. "I try to be strong, to take care of everything and everyone, and I'm so tired of doing it all."

"No one can do it all."

"I have no choice!"

She's hysterical, he decided, at a complete loss as to what to do about it. "OK, OK. Take it easy. You won't have to do it all today."

Standing on her porch, he looked into the tear-drenched green eyes and arched a brow at her. "Do you think you can open the door? I happen to have my hands full."

Shifting in his embrace, Cathy reached down and turned the knob. The door swung open with a squeaky complaint.

Needs oiling, Jared thought, stepping through the doorway. Looking around, he met with three pairs of wide eyes, all in various shades of green and gold.

"What happened?"

"Who are you?"

"Why are you carrying my mama?"

The questions all came at once. Jared answered them in the same manner. "Hurt her foot. She can't walk. Jared. What are your names?"

"Samantha," the oldest child replied.

"Sabrina and Salena," the other two chorused while he carried their mother into the kitchen.

"And this is Samuel." They pointed to the baby who sat in a high-chair playing with his oatmeal instead of eating it.

"Lots of S's." A hint of shock shivered along his spine

at the chaos in front of him.

"Our dad's name was Samuel too."

Must be quite a winner, he thought, wondering what possessed people to give children names based on their initials.

"He died before Sammy was born," Sabrina (or was it Salena?) informed him, making Jared ashamed of his unwarranted thoughts.

"Are you going to be our new daddy?"

He chuckled, surprised at the question. *Out of the mouths of babes...* "Not that I'm aware of. How old are you, Sweetheart?"

"Six."

"Well Miss...?" He waited for her to fill in the blank.

"Sabrina."

"Miss Sabrina. Do you think you can run and get a couple of pillows for your mom's foot?"

Nodding she rushed off.

"We'll need an ice pack too," he informed the other little girl, placing his cargo in a chair and propping up her foot on another one.

"What's an ice pack?" Salena asked.

"In the freezer," Samantha answered, taking care of the baby while keeping one eye on him. "That's it," she assured her sister, when the little girl opened the freezer door and picked up the ice pack with a questioning look.

Sabrina arrived with the pillows. Jared removed Cathy's shoe, noticing the rapid swelling and discoloration of her ankle. Placing the ice pack on it, he surveyed the youngsters. They looked back at him.

Anxious. Expectant.

"What next?" he asked Cathy.

She sighed, closed her eyes for a moment and took a deep breath. "The baby needs to be cleaned up and changed. The twins need to be dressed, and their hair brushed. Lunches have to be prepared, and the dishes put in the dishwasher..." She broke off, looking as if she were trying to stifle a smile. No doubt the incredulity he felt was reflected on his face.

No way, Jared thought. She'd listed nearly a dozen chores to be accomplished in the span of sixty minutes. He consulted his watch. *Seventy max.* Squaring his shoulders, he assumed the authoritative stance he learned during twenty years in the Navy, faced the four helpless creatures before him, and delegated duties.

"Samantha, change the baby and then get yourself ready. Girls show me your room, and I'll help you pick out your clothes. You can dress yourselves, can't you?" He sighed with relief when they nodded.

Cathy smiled at him when he returned. "I think we got off on the wrong foot this morning. At least I did."

She eyed her foot with a rueful frown and held out a hand in greeting. "I'm Cathy Johnson."

"Jared Savoy." He shook the proffered hand, noting how her eyes sparkled when she smiled.

After cleaning and changing the baby, Samantha brought him to her mother then hurried to get dressed and help the twins while Jared prepared lunches.

He handed Cathy a glass of juice. "You do this every day?"

"This is just the beginning."

* * *

Whew! Jared thought, backing the ancient station wagon out of the garage an hour and a half later. *And I thought my day was tough.* In less time than it took him to network an entire office system, he'd managed—just barely—to get three children ready for school, lunches prepared for all of them, dishes done, and a toddler buckled into his car seat. Now, with their mother as navigator, they were on their way. After which, he intended, despite her protests, to get Ms. Cathy Johnson to a doctor.

Returning to her house shy of noon, he carried her in once more, this time to the couch, and went out to retrieve the sleeping child. Laying Samuel in his playpen, he poured Cathy a glass of water and administered over-the-counter medicine for relief of her discomfort.

A mild sprain, the doctor had informed them. Nothing a couple of days rest wouldn't cure. Jared had taken it upon himself to provide crutches that would enable her to move around more easily.

"Lunch." He served the hamburgers and french-fries he'd picked up on the way home. "Is there anything else I can do?"

"Well, now that you mention it..." She hesitated.

"What? Your wish is my command."

They'd learned a lot about each other in four short hours. She was a widow. He'd never been married. Both were incredibly busy, and neither were totally happy with their circumstances. But faith in God enabled them to make the most of their perspective lives.

Cathy nodded toward the desk. "That work needs to be dropped off. More will be waiting. I usually do that while I'm out in the mornings but, with this mishap, we were running late. Then dinner has to be prepared. I try to cook early so I can help the children with their homework and school projects. And the kids have to be picked up at three."

Jared gathered the two huge manila envelopes off the desk. "What kind of work is it?"

"Office notes for a physician and a deposition for an attorney. Their addresses are there with the material. I do medical and legal transcription here at home, as well as business writing, reports, and other desktop publishing projects. It's how I help support my family."

He gazed at her in amazement. "You do all of this every day?"

She nodded.

"No wonder you escape for a run in the mornings."

"I've no choice. It's really not that hard when you're organized. Working from home enables me to spend quality time with my children, make a decent living, and not have to put Sammy in daycare or leave him with a baby-sitter. This ankle threw a monkey wrench in my organized little world though."

He grinned. "I'd say so."

Following her instructions, Jared provided her with the things she'd need to occupy the baby while he was gone and then took off to run errands for her. Dinner was another subject altogether, he thought. They'd have to settle for pizza. He and the girls picked up two frozen ones on the way home along with the makings of a green salad.

* * *

Later that evening, a sigh rose up from within her when Cathy sank chin deep into the hot bath prepared for her. The kids were fed, bathed and ready for bed. Samantha had cleaned the kitchen while Jared read a story to the twins. Sammy had fallen asleep almost immediately after supper, worn out by the rough-and-tumble entertainment Jared provided, after propping Cathy up at the desk, where she'd managed to get some work done.

Heat infused her face and eher chest thinking about Jared... The long expanse of his legs and well-muscled thighs. His narrow waist, broad chest, and wide shoulders topped by an incredibly handsome face complete with quirky smile and dancing brown eyes.

Be still my heart. She placed a hand over the mad thumping in her chest. Rising from the tub, she forced her thoughts into some semblance of order and dried off.

Wrapping herself in a thick, terrycloth robe, she brushed out her honey-colored hair and hobbled into the girls' room to kiss them goodnight.

Escorting Jared to the door, she thanked him for all he'd done. It wasn't until she was snug in her bed that she realized her prayer had been answered. God had sent her an angel. She giggled and drifted off to dream heavenly dreams.

* * *

Cathy had offered the use of her car, but Jared opted to walk home, even though he was exhausted. Pleasantly so, he realized. He'd never had so much fun in his life. Being a bachelor at thirty-eight was not a choice for him, but a self-imposed sentence. Orphaned at birth, he'd often dreamed of having a big family. That dream was shattered when he learned he could not father a child. At the news, he'd refrained from permanent, complicated relationships. Now he wondered if God was showing him there was always a way to have your dreams and desires, as long as it was *His* way.

He stayed up late that night praying and working in the house. The next morning, he jogged over to Cathy's to lend a helping hand once more. Sounds of chaos and laughter could be heard from within, bringing a smile to his lips. He knocked.

His heart hammered in his chest when Cathy answered the door on the edge of a laugh, her eyes glittering with amusement.

"Morning."

"Morning."

He grinned. "Sounds like a party going on in there."

She chuckled. "Just normal morning chaos."

He resisted the urge to kiss those smiling lips.

"Thought I'd run over and give you a hand."

Cathy swung the door open and hobbled out of his way. "A helping hand is nice."

She winked at him and his heart skipped a thud. "A pair is even better."

He fought the urge to kiss her again, laughed instead, and followed her into the kitchen.

As he had the day before, Jared took control, delegated duties, and had everyone ready and out of the door, this time with twenty minutes to spare. He stayed the whole day, playing with the baby and helping where he could, then took it upon himself to do a few minor house repairs. Oiling doors, caulking windows, fixing leaky faucets, replacing loose or broken steps. He and Cathy laughed and talked, their conversations heightened by sensual undercurrents, the brush of hands, and long, lingering gazes.

By the time he left that evening, Jared knew he'd found God's will for his life. He promised himself that if she looked at him tomorrow, the way she'd looked at him today, he wouldn't hesitate to sample the flavor and texture of her mouth.

Three days later, Samantha surprised him when she asked him to take them to the mall. "Sunday is Mother's Day. Daddy used to take us, and we haven't been able to give her anything but homemade gifts since he died."

Jared called Cathy so she wouldn't worry. Telling her he had a couple of errands to run, he assured her the kids wouldn't be a bother. He took the three girls on an unlimited shopping spree, refusing to let them spend the allowance they'd been saving for years. He agreed to hide the treasures at his house and surprise Cathy on Sunday.

Bright and early Sunday morning, he arrived in time to help Samantha with breakfast and getting the children ready for church. After the service, where all mothers were honored, he took the family for an extravagant lunch at the ritziest restaurant in town.

Jared pulled her car into Cathy's garage and helped her into the house. Samantha carried Sammy. Sabrina and Salena retrieved the gifts he'd stashed in his trunk that morning. They were opened amidst laughter and tears that filled Jared's heart with a sense of joy and purpose he'd never experienced before, and he knew he'd found the family he'd always wanted.

Over the next few weeks, he prayed, planned and prepared.

* * *

Cathy relished Jared's visits. Long before he returned to work, they slipped into a routine— a morning run together, and then each embarked on their daily obligations. Evenings were for quiet conversation, tender kisses and teasing caresses.

Days turned into weeks. Weeks slid into a month and still, Jared was always there when she needed him the most. He'd become adept at fixing lunches, brushing hair and entertaining a toddler—very adept. Strong and reliable, gentle, and kind, he was also proving to be an excellent go-fer, a marvelous masseur and a superb kisser. The soft, sensual feel of his lips on hers, the gentle touch of his hands, and sweet words he whispered made Cathy feel cherished, secure, and sexy.

Things she hadn't felt in years.

They were sitting on the porch swing one June evening beneath a beautiful starlit sky when she confessed her prayer on that not-so-long-ago, and definitely not-forgotten, morning when they first met.

"A well-trained angel, huh?" He brushed his lips across hers in a gentle caress.

Cathy nodded unable to speak for the need clamoring in her throat. "Even if only for a day," she croaked, grateful God had blessed her with more than one day with this particular angel, and yet afraid to even hope or dream for a single day more.

Putting his arm around her shoulder, Jared gazed into her brilliant green gaze. He lifted her hand to his lips. "Only for a day?"

Her heart stuttered. She gazed into his face. "What do you mean?"

Jared withdrew a ring from his shirt pocket. "How about an angel for life?"

His lips captured hers in a kiss ripe with passion and promise.

Her children cheered. Their enthusiasm assured Cathy saying anything other than yes was not an option.

Three weeks later she and the kids made sure Jared's first Father's Day celebration was one he'd remember and cherish for life.

The End

Dear Reader,

Although Cathy and Jared's lives are not exactly how they planned, their faith in God allows them to manage quite nicely and yet, stay open to His will. In the end, both of their dreams come true as a result of obedience and trust.

If you don't know Him already, I pray that you too, will pursue a relationship with the Lord Jesus and if you do, that you will call upon Him in your time of trouble, for He will hear and answer.

As always, may God bless and keep you—and yours—in the palm of His mighty hand!

Detained for Love

Fourth of July decorations lined the streets as the town prepared for the annual holiday. Soon it would be overrun with returning natives, as well as tourists, pouring in for the carnival, parade, and fireworks. Madeline cringed when she saw the police cruiser and automatically glanced at her speedometer while pressing on the brakes. Her worst fears came to life when he hit the siren and lights, made a U-turn, and pulled up behind her.

She navigated her car to the side of the road, took several deep breaths, rolled her window down and pasted a smile on her face as he approached. Her father's advice rang in her ears, tugged at her heart: *Always smile. Never get defensive. Police don't have time and know better than to stop anyone without probable cause.*

"Good morning, officer."

"Driver's license, registration and proof of insurance please."

Maddy gathered the requested items and handed them to him.

"Do you know why I stopped you, Ms. ...?" He glanced down at her license, then back. "Albright."

"No, sir."

"You were doing 48 in a 35."

Maddy frowned. "I thought the speed limit was 45, Officer...?"

"Roberts. Speed limit switched to 35 at the four-way

stop."

Maddy groaned. "I honestly didn't know that. I travel this road all the time and never noticed the change."

"Wait here, please."

Like I have a choice Maddy thought and watched him walk back to his cruiser through her side mirror. She sent a swift, silent plea heavenward that her spotless driving record would grant her a bit of grace. She fidgeted in her seat, snapped the seatbelt against her shoulder and glanced in her rearview mirror as Officer Roberts disembarked from his car and walked toward her again.

"I'll let you go with a warning, Ms. Albright, but pay a little more attention. Next time, you might not be so lucky."

"Thank you! I truly appreciate your kindness, and I thank you for your service. My dad was a police officer."

His eyes softened when her voice wobbled on 'was.'

They exchanged pleasantries another minute then went their separate ways. An hour later, Maddy rushed through the post office door and bumped headlong into Officer Roberts again.

"Still in a hurry, I see." His smile took the sting out of the comment.

Warmth flooded her cheeks. Excitement fluttered in her stomach. "My dad always said I have two speeds: stop and wide open."

He eyed her for a moment. "You'll enjoy your day so much more if you slow down a bit. Might help you ease up on that accelerator too."

Maddy smiled. "Just trying to beat the crowds and finish my errands before everything shuts down for the fair tonight and 4th of July festivities this weekend, but I'll keep that in mind."

He nodded. "Good."

Though she could stand there all day, lost in his gaze, Maddy eased away. "Well, guess I shouldn't keep you from your duties any longer."

His eyes laughed and mocked and didn't miss a thing. "No hardship on my part to be detained by a pretty lady."

A tiny shiver of pleasure raced over her arms. Maddy thanked him and continued towards her car on legs that wobbled.

Later that evening, Maddy relaxed in a hot bath with a cup of tea and thought about the handsome officer with his expressive green eyes. She'd barely had time to dry off and pull on jeans and a sweatshirt when her doorbell pealed.

"Who in the world?" She rushed to the foyer and opened the door. Her eyes widened in surprise. A gasp stuck in her throat.

As though conjured by her thoughts, Officer Roberts stood on her porch.

Mirth lit his features. His eyes shone with glee. A smile tugged at his lips. Yet, he regarded her with a solemn shake of his head. "Didn't even find out who was at your door before flinging it open. Didn't your police officer father teach you to be a little more cautious? Especially when the town is inundated with carnival folks, tourists and strangers in for the holiday?"

Her lips curved. "He tried. Taught me self-defense and martial arts instead."

"Good job, dad." He laughed, then held a wallet toward her.

She reached for it. "I... uh... Thank you?"

"Jacob. Evidently you dropped it when you nearly ran me over at the post office. I found it by the curb. Since there's no phone number or emergency contact information in there, I didn't know how else to reach you. I passed by here a couple of times, but you weren't home. I saw your car in the drive this time and figured I'd get this to you before you were stopped and in trouble for driving without a license."

"Do you always go above and beyond even when not on duty?" she asked, noting for the first time he was not in uniform.

"It's my job to serve, Ma'am."

Maddy tucked her wallet into her back pocket and grabbed her keys off the hook by the door. "How about I treat you to a cup of coffee or tea for your trouble? Unless you have somewhere to be? I wouldn't want to keep you from your plans."

He chuckled and offered his arm. "Already said it's no hardship to be detained by a pretty lady."

The End

Dear Reader,

Many of you may know, my beloved Terry was a Law Enforcement Officer. I wrote this story with him in mind. Like our hero Jacob, he often went above and beyond the call of duty when necessary and he taught our children the same lesson Maddy's father taught her...

Always smile. Never get defensive. Police don't have time and know better than to stop anyone without probable cause.

Perhaps you'll keep that in mind the next time you get pulled over or snagged at a traffic stop.

Praying for a little grace never hurts either.

If you don't know HIM already, I pray you will seek a personal relationship with the Lord, Jesus Christ and if you do, that you'll continue to draw closer to Him and in all things you will give Him praise.

Ferryn's Quest

Ferryn closed her eyes, said a prayer, and sent the resume into cyberspace. Pinpricks of excitement traveled along every cell and nerve. Stepping away from the computer, she emitted a little laugh then twirled in front of the mirror in her dance costume. A full-skirted white dress with fitted top. Brightly colored sash encircled her waist. Matching scarves adorned her hair and around her throat. Boots, and a white hat whose band reflected the colors in her attire, completed her ensemble.

A smile curved her lips, brightened her eyes, and caused color to bloom in her cheeks. Doubt wasn't permitted. Only optimism, unerring faith, and profound gratitude, all of which she called the magic of life. That magic rose in her breast, pumped through her blood.

She would get this, or her name wasn't Ferryn.

And there, she would find him.

If someone asked how she knew, she couldn't tell. Only that she did. It wasn't a lover she sought or a mate. She didn't have time for either. She had too much to do, too many places to see.

Too many questions to answer.

No, Ferryn didn't need a lover or a mate to fulfill an already abundant life. But a father.

Her father.

She knew who he was, where he last resided. What she didn't know was why he always managed to stay one step, one port, ahead of her. He'd been named after a country singer and she, after him.

Both embodied the meaning of the title: wanderer, adventurous, gypsy.

She had his coloring—raven hair, cobalt eyes. And her mother's build—tiny frame, pixie-like features.

But she'd grown up without either.

Her mother died in childbirth. Distraught, heartbroken, her father left. Walked away and never looked back. At least, that's what Ferryn wanted to believe, chose to believe, despite her maternal grandmother's ranting otherwise.

Grandmother had told Ferryn to forget him. To not waste her life looking for a man who didn't have the intestinal fortitude to stand up against grief and raise his daughter. One who didn't have a responsible bone in his body or an ounce of permanency in his DNA.

Ferryn didn't buy that. How could she when his blood ran through her veins?

So, she prayed and meditated. Searched and found and followed him. Through mountains and woods. Across rivers and lakes. Beyond seas and oceans. Spanning continents. And she'd seen him in her dreams... Huddled under a darkened fishing pier in Alaska. Playing guitar on the beach in St Croix. In her fantasies he was always the same handsome young man who'd conceived a child with his fairy maiden. Only in her dreams were they together. Always and only together.

A knock on her door interrupted Ferryn's musing.

"Five minutes, Ms. Guilliot."

Ferryn smoothed her bodice, ran impatient fingers through her hair and swiped color on her lips to match the brightest swatch in her scarves. One more week, a month at most, and she'd be off this ship and on board another cruise line bound for ports known and unknown in the South Pacific.

* * *

Wendell Carrier waited for his cue as his dance partner slid into her spot beside him mere moments before they were due on stage. Pretty Ferryn Guilliot with her ruby lips, deep blue eyes, and alabaster skin. And magic feet. He mustn't forget the magic feet. Lithe and graceful, the woman could move like no other he'd seen or danced with before.

Was it any wonder he was madly in love?

Two years her senior they grew up in the same quiet neighborhood in a tiny, backwoods, southeast Texas town. She snagged his attention the first time he saw her out dancing and playing in her back yard and captured his heart the evening of his senior prom. He left town after graduation to attend the community college in a nearby city. They'd stayed in touch, but a bit shy and insecure, Wendell never told Ferryn of his feelings for her. She seemed too ambitious to settle for a small town boy.

Besides, Ferryn was on a mission and nothing, or no one, would stand in her way.

Her first job as a flight attendant right out of high

school almost killed him. He watched and waited and wondered if she'd ever come back. When she did, he determined to never let her out of his sight again. Always up for an adventure, she switched careers and locations, moving more often than his military family had his entire life. And it always relieved him when she came back. When she stopped bouncing long enough to settle as a dancer/performer with this cruise line, he followed.

Ship to ship, and port to port, they'd danced together ever since.

Tonight was no different. Wendell held her in his arms and waltzed and twirled and square danced as the show progressed from the first number to the finale'. Fueled by adrenaline, he grabbed her hand and rushed offstage then pulled her into an exuberant embrace. His lips grazed her cheek. "We did it again, pretty Ferryn. Listen to that crowd!"

She beamed. "Meet you on deck as usual?"

He nodded then promenaded with her back out onto the stage to take their final bows. A half-hour later, freshly showered and famished, he raided the buffet, piled a plate full of finger foods—what he didn't stuff in his mouth along the way—and then joined Ferryn on deck. He stopped for a moment, stunned by her beauty.

Pulled up into a pony tail, her rich, sable hair scattered in the breeze. Her skin, free of makeup, glowed luminously in the evening light. A white T-shirt clung like a second skin over the smooth curve of her shoulders, the strong torso, and disappeared into jeans that hugged her hips and outlined slim, firm thighs. A thin belt glittered at her waist and matched the sparkle in her eyes when she turned to smile at him.

Her scent perfumed the air, whispered to his senses. Wendell closed the distance between them with a few solid strides. He pressed a kiss to her forehead, took her hand and led her to a table and chairs nearby then placed the plate between them. Ravenous, Ferryn dug in. A waiter passed by, offered them a beverage. Wendell chose a glass of wine for each of them and joined her in demolishing the food.

Her hunger appeased, Ferryn sat back with a sigh and sipped. "I applied for another ship today."

Wendell closed his eyes and suppressed a groan. Typical, he thought, always another ship. "Where to this time?"

"The Oceania area. I requested a position for both of us."

She hadn't even bothered to ask or discuss it with him, just assumed he'd tag along.

Why should she? That's what you've always done. Wendell sipped his wine and bit back on the frustration that rose to choke him. He questioned, and not for the first time, his reasons, his sanity, at traipsing after her all over the world. "Oceania? You mean Australia, New Zealand, and Malaysia."

She smiled and the breath backed up in his lungs. "Fiji, the Philippines, and Honolulu."

Wendell grinned. "How romantic. But why? Or need I ask."

Ferryn closed her eyes, breathed deep. "I see–feel–

him there, Wendell. And this time I'll find him. Meet him. Get to know him."

"And have all those questions answered."

She nodded. "I know it's hard for some to understand. Especially someone who was raised in the security of a generous, loving family. I need to do this. I need to know who I am. And I need to know why my life was not important enough for him to stay. Why I was deserted."

It still astonished him, this sixth sense of hers. Amazed and irritated at the same time. Astounded that she somehow *knew* where her father was, frustrated that he always seemed to be one step ahead of her. Like he knew she was chasing him and didn't want to be caught. "What makes you so sure you'll actually meet him this time?"

Ferryn shrugged. "I just know. It's time, don't you think?"

"Past time if you ask me. I'd love to see you find peace about all of this and settle down some."

A tiny smile tugged at her pretty bow shaped mouth and added glitter to her already bright eyes. "What makes you think I'll settle down after finding him?"

Wendell chortled. "One can only hope."

She turned to him fully, her face serious. "What do you want from me, Wendell?"

He leaned closer and brushed his lips across hers. "You. All of you, pretty Ferryn. Peaceful. Whole. And free from the things that haunt you."

"But why?"

He cupped her face in his palm, traced her mouth with his thumb then replaced it with his. Everything he felt poured into the kiss.

Ferryn's heart stumbled then jumped into overdrive. Her blood warmed by degrees and thudded through her veins in thick, slow waves. She shifted in his arms as hers slipped around his neck. Her hands fisted in his hair, and she melted into his strong embrace.

Whole. Complete. She felt all those things in this moment, and in the next several, cuddled against Wendell's chest after the kiss ended. But the questions still lingered. Unanswered and longing for closure on a childhood that, although not bad, was not really good either.

Few people knew of the pain and struggle Ferryn grew up with. She hadn't let on about the negativity which surrounded her every day, or how it stifled and suffocated her spirit. Her grandmother, a bitter old woman, did her level best to destroy or at least tame the wandering trait she'd inherited from her parents. And the need for freedom and creative expression. She'd been boxed, cornered and all but shoved into conformity.

But a free spirit will always break away from restraint.

And that's exactly what Ferryn did the day she graduated high school. And now, at twenty-six, she still felt the kick of panic—though not as hard—at being trapped or confined to one place. One person. Though Wendell shared many of her dreams and desires to travel, and to dance, he was more grounded than she.

Ferryn knew he wanted the traditional home and family. His chuckle jerked her mind from its wanderings.

She eased away, glanced up at him. "What's so funny?"

He grinned and brushed a hand over her hair. "I know you too well, pretty Ferryn. I can hear the gears turning in that head of yours, feel your resistance, and assure you once again, my sweet, that I have no desire to fence you in. A home and family doesn't have to be a jail sentence."

Ferryn cocked her head and grinned at him. "Perhaps you do know me too well."

He rose, held a hand down to help her up. "Yep. Just like I know it's time for you to get to bed. You'll be grumpy in the morning without your customary eight to ten hours of sleep."

This time it was she who giggled. "As will you."

* * *

Faren Guilliot walked to the edge of the peer and gazed out over Wellington Harbour just as the sun began to set in a wild display of bleeding colors and fading light. He stayed until the moon rose in its place.

Shuffling his guitar and backpack, he folded himself into a sitting position then pulled out a well-worn sleeping bag and stretched out under the stars. The featherdown lining would provide warmth against the evening chill and the vinyl exterior, protection from the morning dew.

This wasn't the first night he'd slept outside. Wouldn't be the last. Although he feared his wandering days were coming to an end. He'd have to settle somewhere soon. He gazed up at the night sky, counting the tiny lights twinkling on and off in the heavens. One flared and burned out as it shot toward the earth. Faren closed his eyes and made a wish. The same wish he'd made for years.

A wish he knew wouldn't come true.

Not yet anyway.

Faren knew he'd have to tie up loose ends before he'd be granted passage to the other side of life. A sigh of exasperation ripped from his tight chest when his daughter's face rose in his mind. A tear trickled from the corner of his eye.

He'd let her find him this time.

He knew Ferryn looked for him. Had always known. He saw her in his dreams, felt when she got too close. Not willing to face the years of loss and regret—the years of heartache—he'd always stayed ahead of her. But time was drawing near now, and he could, *would* face her. He'd make amends as best he could before time ran out.

Before he died.

The tightness in his chest eased. Faren gazed up at the stars again, had his nightly commune with God, then drifted to sleep.

A bright light and harsh voice, followed by a swift kick, woke him some hours later.

"Hey! Get up you old fool and get moving before I haul you in."

Faren struggled his way out of the sleeping bag and rolled it up. He didn't bother to answer, much less argue, or defy. Years of experience had taught him none of those tactics worked. He simply tucked the sleeping bag into his backpack, shouldered it and his guitar, and then vacated the pier.

Later that morning, Faren dug enough coins and bills out of his pocket to buy a shower at the nearest truck stop and breakfast at a restaurant with a patio for dining near the water.

"Well, hello, and how are you this fine morning?"

The sultry voice caused his pulse to quicken. Faren looked up at the waitress and the breath backed up in his lungs. A shiver rattled his soul. *It couldn't be!* He shook his head, sipped coffee, and took a second glance, relieved to see the age difference between this one and his beloved Christyl.

A frown creased her brow. "Are you OK?"

Faren smiled and nodded. "You remind me of someone I once knew. Startled me there for a moment."

Her eyebrow arched in curiosity. "Old flame?"

"Something like that."

"Well, I'm sorry I rattled you. What'll you have?"

Faren ordered his customary breakfast of eggs, toast, bacon, coffee, juice, milk and pancakes. He watched the tourists come and go in the shops along the waterfront while he waited. The waitress brought his meal which he ate in meticulous order. Eggs, bacon, and toast, first, with the juice. Milk with the pancakes.

A memory rose in his mind and caused him to

smile... *He and Christyl sitting at a diner in Wales and the way she laughed over his eating habit.*

He swiped at his eyes just as the waitress appeared to refresh his coffee. "Can I get you anything else?"

"No thanks."

"You know, I've worked here for years and don't believe I've seen you before. New to the area or just passing through?"

Normally Faren avoided such conversations but seeing as he intended on staying a while, he answered her. "New to the area. Know where I can find a boarding house or cheap hotel somewhere near the art district?"

Christyl shook her head. "Not right off. But there's a free paper that lists rentals and such. You might grab one on your way out. Unless you're going to sit a spell. Then I can bring one to you."

Faren tried to ignore the flutter of his heart and the stirring of his blood at the lyrical tone of her voice. "That would be nice. I'm not in a hurry this morning."

She walked away and within a few moments returned with the periodical. Faren smiled and thanked her then buried his nose in the rental section of the classified ads.

Christyl made sure his coffee didn't run out or get cold. Two hours later, Faren left and made his way to the art district a few miles away. Before the end of day, he'd rented a small efficiency apartment not much bigger than the dock he'd slept on the night before. One that, with the exception of food, contained everything he needed to settle in for the remaining months of his life.

* * *

Ferryn raced down the passageway and hurdled up the stairs toward the auditorium. Practice started fifteen minutes ago, and she was late! For the first time in a long time, dreams had robbed her of the sleep her body needed to continue functioning with the same level of energy she usually maintained. Even now, as she exerted what little stamina she had left after the restless night, adrenalin caused by panic kicked in and propelled her onto the dance floor right on cue for the second number. She stopped. Her heart plummeted to her feet.

What's *she* doing in his arms?

Meghan O'Reiley had had a thing for Wendell as long as they'd been on this ship. She hadn't been subtle about it either.

Ferryn backed off the stage, sank down onto a step in the stairwell and waited until that particular dance practice ended.

Ms. Fournerat, the Director/Choreographer called for a timeout then summoned Ferryn onto the stage. "You requested another assignment, Ms. Guilliot?"

Ferryn felt the chastisement in her tone. "Yes, Ma'am. But not until after Labor Day."

A stern nod followed by, "Pack your things then. You'll disembark at the next port. Ms. O'Reiley will take your spot until the tour, and *your* contract, are fulfilled."

Ferryn's eyes met Wendell's in question but before he could answer, Meghan slipped her arm through his and purred.

Wendell disengaged Meghan's arm and turned his back to her. "They didn't need me, Ferryn. You'll have to go it alone this time."

Ferryn started to protest but Ms. Fournerat interrupted with a shrill of her whistle. "Discuss it later. Dancers man your positions!"

Meghan tossed a smirk over her shoulder and partnered up with Wendell once more.

Ferryn walked back to her stateroom and began packing. An hour later, she answered a knock on her door.

Wendell strode through, turned, and stroked his hands down her arms in a tender caress. "I'm sorry, Ferryn."

She blinked back the tears and swallowed the hard knot of emotion clogging her throat. "It's not your fault. I just never imagined finding my father and meeting him without you by my side. Wish you could just quit and come with me."

"You know I can't do that. Wouldn't, even if I could. It's bad karma to break a contract or leave someone in a bind."

Ferryn frowned. "The only person you'd leave in a bind is Meghan. Besides, I never intended to break my contract, just to change ships. Which is *why* I requested the switch *after* Labor Day."

"Unfortunately, that's not how some people see it. I don't understand why you couldn't wait until this tour was complete before applying for another ship. At least, then we may have had a better chance of being together."

"You know why. I've got to find him before time runs out."

Wendell snorted. "Where do you get this stuff? What makes you think time is running out? What are you going to do when, if, you find him and he's healthy and whole and simply enjoying his life without you? What if everything your grandmother said all these years is true?"

"I can't believe you'd even think that. My grandmother is a bitter old hag."

Wendell fought the urge to shake her. She'd always had, in his opinion, this unreasonable anger toward her grandmother. "Your grandmother is a good woman whose only daughter died and, instead of being able to enjoy her granddaughter, was thrust into the role of raising a child at her advanced age. On top of that, she was abandoned by the one person who could have given her, given both of you, the help and support necessary to create a loving home and a nurturing environment. It's time you grew up Ferryn and tried to see things from her perspective instead of this fantasy you've built around your father."

She looked as though he'd struck her. For a moment Wendell wished he could take back his words. But he'd refrained from saying them for so long and sometimes, the truth was hard to swallow.

"I never realized you felt that way." Her eyes filled. Voice trembled.

He reached for her.

Ferryn slapped his hands away. "Don't touch me."

"Ferryn…"

She shook her head, cutting off further words. "You've felt like this all along and never said anything? Was your support false? Our relationship built on lies and half-truths?"

Wendell took a deep breath and tried to reason with her. "I do support you! I've never lied to you about my feelings, so no. Our relationship is *not* built on lies and half-truths. But I do believe you're running off half-cocked around the world looking for someone who may not want to be found. Most of the time, you don't think things through or reason them out, you just act on impulse."

"I act on instinct with meditation, prayer and fasting!" She held up a hand. "Just stop. I feel like I don't even know you right now."

A tremble of fear coursed through him at the coldness in her tone. He stepped toward her. "Really? Well, know and remember this…"

He pulled her against him, covered her lips with his before she could protest, and held her tight against his chest until she relaxed against him. Softening the kiss by degrees, he loosened his desperate hold, cuddled her for a moment then trailed his lips in feathery caresses across her cheeks and forehead. Without a word, he released her and left her to finish packing.

* * *

Ferryn disembarked the ship after it docked in Cancun, Mexico then took a taxi to the airport and booked a flight to Wellington, New Zealand where her corresponding ship would be in port, docked for repairs. She had a couple of weeks before the cruiser sailed and, since she'd never been to New Zealand, decided she'd spend that time exploring. While waiting on her flight, she researched the area and booked a room in a B&B near the coast. Between layovers and flight delays, nearly thirty hours passed before she checked into her room.

Tossing her bags on one bed, Ferryn took a long, luxurious shower, then stretched out under the covers of the other, and slept away the rest of her day and long into the next. Jet lag rendered her too tired to do anything but enjoy an afternoon snack followed by dinner with fellow guests at the B&B, but Ferryn determined to get an early start the next morning. She perused brochures of tours and various outings she intended to enjoy during her brief stay.

Switching the device off 'airplane mode', her phone pinged, again and again, as messages from the past couple of days came through. Ferryn responded where necessary then listened to Wendell's voicemail…

"Hey, I know we parted on a sour note, but please let me know when you arrive at your destination safely."

Sour note? Ferryn swiped at the tears that dared to fall. She'd cried enough in the last three days. She hit delete and moved on to the next.

"Ferryn, I know it's a long trip but surely you had at least one layover. Call me."

He sounded more angry than worried. She hit delete again.

A heavy sigh preceded his words this time. "I'm sorry, Ferryn. I know I should have shared my feelings instead of keeping them to myself. Damn, I hate apologizing over the phone. Call me. Please. Or at least text and let me know you're all right."

Not trusting herself if she heard his voice, Ferryn shot a short text informing him she'd arrived and was safe. Before he could respond, her phone rang. The cruise line's main number flashed on her screen. "Hello?"

"Ms. Guilliot?"

"This is she."

"Have you arrived in Wellington Harbour?"

"Yes."

"Good! Our lead dancer broke her ankle. Her alternate just found out she's pregnant and left us. We need you to report ASAP for rehearsal. We've less than two weeks before we set sail and need you to be able to perform in her stead."

"I'll be there in the morning."

"Good. Give us your location and we'll send a car and take care of your bill."

Ferryn relayed her information and hung up with a sigh. "So much for sightseeing or anything else."

The next morning, she met the driver at eight o'clock sharp. Once settled into her cabin below deck of the luxury liner, she hurried to the ballroom where the other dancers chatted while they stretched. The director introduced her to the all-female troupe and walked Ferryn through her routine then practice started.

Sweat, due diligence and hours of going over her routine alone and with the others, ensured Ferryn would be ready when the ship sailed for the first of back to back, 14 day cruises with a mere 3 day break between over New Zealand's Labour Day weekend.

After practice, Ferryn spent each night on deck alone. She hadn't realized until this time away from him, how much she'd grown to love her time with Wendell. She knew his tour had been extended a month past America's Labor Day weekend, and he'd given notice that he was leaving once it finished but, other than that, their schedules and the difference in time zones afforded them few opportunities to speak.

Her maiden voyage with the ensemble went off without a hitch, as did the two that followed. Tired of nearly eight weeks of ship cuisine, Ferryn hurried to a dockside café whose menu boasted burgers, chips and thick shakes. Grabbing a table on the patio, she smiled at the waitress who appeared with a glass of water. Waving away the laminated list of options, Ferryn ordered.

"Can I get you an entrée while you wait? We're pretty busy with folks being off for Labour Day *and* the tourists, so it'll be a while before your dinner is ready."

"I'll have the Caramelized Macadamia Nuts, please."

Five minutes later Ferryn thanked the server then looked up at her quizzically when the woman hesitated.

"Have we met before?"

Ferryn eyed her closely. "I don't think so. This is my

first visit here. I work on the cruise ship."

Christyl—according to her nametag—frowned. "You just seem so familiar."

Ferryn shrugged.

"Oh well, I'll bring your dinner as soon as it's ready."

"Thank you."

Nearly an hour later, Cristyl brought out her meal. Ferryn sank her teeth and hummed in appreciation at the first taste of fatty red meat she'd had in months. Savoring each bite, she finished up and then left a generous tip with her ticket. Two days later she set sail again without seeing anything other than the harbour during their break.

* * *

Faren sat on the balcony of his apartment and watched the tourists and cruise ship employees flow onto the pier and into town. Sunshine bounced off the water in a blinding glare, but he welcomed the warmth. *So much brighter than that dismal hospital room.*

He'd been home for two days after a month-long stay in the telemetry ward, where they'd run every test in the book, only to tell him what he already knew.

He was dying of a broken heart.

As he had been for years.

Hearing her key in the door, telltale knock, and Crystle calling, "Youhoo, hello!" Faren sent up a silent 'thank you' that she cared enough to keep checking on him. In fact, had it not been for her calling nine-one-one, he may not be here today. Which is why he'd given her the key.

She placed a hand on his shoulder. "How are you feeling?"

Faren smiled. "Enjoying the sunshine."

She bent down and kissed his cheek. "Good. Your color is back. Have you been for your walk yet?"

"No."

"You've got to take better care of yourself." Her voice held a note of sadness. A hint of wistfulness.

Faren squeezed her hand and held on to it as she sat down across from him.

"You've made me happier than I've been in years, sweet Crystle. But I haven't had the desire to live since my wife died."

She jerked her hand from his. "Well, you're not going to die on my watch. What about your daughter? Surely she's worth living for. Speaking of..."

She peered closely at him. Scrutinizing.

Faren waited, eyebrow arched in question.

"A young woman came into the diner today. She seemed so familiar, but I couldn't place her. Do you have a picture of your wife or daughter?"

Faren's heart quickened. *Dare he hope?* Digging the faded photograph out of his beat up, old wallet, he handed it to her.

Crystal's eyes widened. "Maybe... I don't know. There's some resemblance but this is so old and ... I just don't know. I'd hate to get your hopes up."

"Do you know where she lives?"

Crystle shook her head. "She works on one of the cruise ships. I don't know which one but I'm sure she'll be back at some point."

"Do you think we can find out?"

"Would it make a difference? Why would you want to meet her in person and then leave her again. This time for all eternity?"

"I need to make amends."

"You can do that with a letter or phone call. If you're asking me, you are just being a selfish jerk."

Faren winced. The edge in her voice echoed the convictions in his heart. "You're right. But God won't take me until I do."

"Maybe *God* doesn't want to take you at all. Maybe *He* wants you to live. What would your wife think of you acting this way all these years?"

Faren closed his eyes and faced the truth buried deep in his heart. "She wouldn't think very highly of it. Or me."

Crystle leaned forward and cupped his cheeks in her hands. "She would want you to live and be happy and enjoy your grandchildren when they come along. It's what *all* of our loved ones who've passed desire most for us. Anything less is dishonoring their memory."

Faren knew from the conversations they'd had over the last three months, Crystle had survived her own share of grief and loss, which had catapulted her into a spiritual quest for the deeper meanings of life and eternity. And now, when not working at the diner, she used her vast knowledge, experience and empathetic gifts and skills to help others deal with the same situations.

Tiny though it was, a flicker of hope flared alongside the sadness that had bound his heart for so long. *Maybe she was right. Maybe I should think about living more than dying.* He reached for her hand and stood, pulling her up with him. "Let's take that walk, shall we?"

* * *

"Ms. Guilliot."

Ferryn turned as the dance director entered the workout room where she'd been stretching. "Yes, ma'am?"

"A courier brought this message for you. Our lead dancer is back, hale and hearty. She's been practicing at home for the last week or so and is ready to take over her spot. We can find another troupe for you, if you'd like."

Ferryn took the envelope and tucked it into the pocket of her yoga pants. "I'm glad she's healthy but no, thanks. I believe I'll take a couple of weeks off before finding another position." *And do what?*

Ferryn ignored the question that had been rolling around in her head since they docked.

"No worries. We've reserved a room for two nights at the same B&B you stayed in when you arrived. Your final check will be direct deposited within 72 hours. I'll send along a letter of recommendation within that time frame as well."

Ferryn hugged this lady who'd become her favorite of all the dance directors she'd worked with. "Thank you.

I'll remove my things."

"No rush. We don't leave for another two hours."

Knowing if she were the lead dancer, she'd want her space ASAHP and that it needed to be cleaned, Ferryn hurried to gather her belongings and vacate the room she'd occupied for the past eight weeks.

She stopped several times on her way off the ship to say goodbye to fellow performers, staff and crew. Once on shore, she unfolded the note she'd stuck in her pocket over an hour ago.

Ms. Guilliot, please come to the diner when you return to Wellington Harbour. There's someone I'd like you to meet. Thanks! Crystle.

Crystle met her at the door. "Thanks for coming."

"No problem. Your note piqued my curiosity."

"Remember I said you seemed familiar?"

Ferryn nodded.

"Come with me." Crystle led her toward a corner table by the window where a man sat. Alone.

He turned.

Ferryn's heart began to thrum. Blood pounded in her ears. She gasped and raised trembling fingers to her lips. She tried to speak but had to clear the hard knot of emotion clogging her throat. "Daddy?"

They embraced, sobbing, laughing and jabbering at the same time. They talked for hours. Through coffee, dinner and dessert. They were still chatting when Crystle's shift ended, and she joined them.

Faren told of his travels and how he'd somehow felt her following him and apologized for abandoning her.

"How's your grandmother?"

"She's a stern old lady who doesn't understand me and hates you."

"Can't blame her. You shouldn't be so hard on her though."

"I've been telling her that for years."

All three of them turned toward the voice.

"And you are?" Faren wanted to know.

"Wendell Carrier. I've been in love with your daughter since I was ten years old." His eyes never left Ferryn's. "I've come to bring you home, Ferryn. Your grandmother is not doing well."

Ferryn felt the blood drain from her face.

"You should go."

Ferryn shook her head at her father's suggestion. "But I've just found you! Come with me."

"I doubt she wants to see me."

Crystle placed a hand on Faren's arm. "You said you wanted to make amends. Seems like the trip back to America will give you plenty of time to catch up with your daughter and figure out how to do that with your mother-in-law."

"Will you come along as well?"

Crystle smiled. "No. This is something you need to do for yourself. And your family. But I'll be here when you get back."

* * *

Six months later her father, grandmother and

Crystle stood in attendance as Ferryn and Wendell said vows on the dock in Wellington Harbour.

The End

Dear Reader,

Whether literally or figuratively how often do we run away, and hurt those we love most? We try to escape from responsibilities, grief, bad choices, and regrets, not realizing until we face these things head on, we'll never truly find peace. In this story, both Ferryn and her father share a "sixth sense" about each other but the truth is we **all** have this ability to connect on a spiritual and energetic level with others.

Think about it... How many times have you thought about an old friend or someone you haven't talked to in a while, and they call? Or you receive a letter or text or actually run into them somewhere? Quantum Physicists call this 'entanglement.' But what it really is, is that on the spiritual/energetic level we are all connected. We are all one. Think about this the next time you're tempted to run away instead of facing whatever emotions are haunting you.

Stand up. Take responsibility. Pray, meditate, fast, commune with God and your loved ones in your heart. Feel them in your sphere and know that love, grace, forgiveness and gratitude cover a multitude of errors.

Something to think about!
"Inspirational with an Edge!" ™

PS: I purposely spelled Harbour and Labour to honor the setting of Ferryn's Quest.

Kaylyn's Flowers

Never should have looked outside.

Aghast, Kaylyn Joubert stared at the sight before her. Limbs and branches lay strewn about her yard like sentinels downed in battle. Ghosts, goblins and all sorts of Halloween decorations tangled in the trees and mangled her shrubs. On top of that, it appeared as though a twister had picked up the neighbors' trash cans and dumped their contents on top of the carnage.

"Connor!"

Her teenage son bounded down the stairs, then stood for half a minute, mouth open, eyes wide. "Oh man, what a mess."

"Call your coach and let him know you're not coming to practice. It'll take us all day and then some to clear this up."

Connor grumbled all the way to his room.

Kaylyn did the same on her way to the kitchen.

Next to Connor, her flowers were her pride and joy and worth every hour of blood, sweat and tears she invested in tending them. Sowing, reaping, and weeding her garden had helped heal the rents in her heart after her husband's death.

Nurturing the tender bulbs year after year and season upon season gave her life meaning and purpose and cemented the dream of a thriving business in her heart. An avenue through which she could share her love and knowledge of plants with the world one patio garden or miniscule greenhouse at a time.

As Kaylyn gathered the things she needed for breakfast, her phone rang.

"Good morning!" Butterflies danced in her core when Coach Jake Simpson's voice sounded over the line "Heard the wind fairies paid you a visit."

The thought of her demolished flower beds made her heart weep. She swallowed the lump that rose to choke her and dodged the grief with an attempt at humor. "More like wind witches if my yard's any indication."

His chuckle upped the butterflies' waltz to a frenzied Mambo. "We'll be there within the hour to clean up."

"We?"

"I sent a group text after Connor called, canceled practice and asked for a few volunteers to help with cleanup. Our assistant coach and a couple of team dads are doing the same elsewhere across town. It's the least we can do for the way this community supports our boys."

"That's wonderful, Jake! Teaches them the importance of service too. I'll make breakfast."

"No, we want to get right to work, but refreshments after would be appreciated."

"Done." Kaylyn disconnected and danced a little jig across the kitchen floor.

Widowed seven years, she'd doubted her ability to get over the grief and conquer her innate shyness enough to date or fall in love again. Besides, she'd been too busy building her floristry business, finishing her degrees in Botany and Horticulture, and raising her son to consider romance.

Until she met Jake Simpson.

Like a love-struck teen, she'd had a huge crush on him since Connor's first day of football practice.

Humming, she set about making breakfast then pulled out ingredients for pastries, hot chocolate, and her favorite beverage, café mocha. Her mind circled around the man who'd snagged her heart months ago, and the many conversations they'd shared since. They never seemed to run out of things to talk about. The occasional brush of hands and long, lingering looks that sometimes passed between them made her wonder…

Were his feelings for her deeper than simple friendship?

She and Connor had finished eating and the first batch of strawberry and cream-cheese crescents were in the oven when the doorbell rang.

He's here!

Pans clattered in the sink.

Connor pushed away from the table, brought his dishes to Kaylyn, and nudged her with his shoulder. "Should I get that, or do you want a minute to ogle Coach Simpson?"

Kaylyn's cheeks flamed. Laughing, her son evaded the elbow she jabbed at his ribs and headed out. His boots and the cheerful tune he whistled echoed the cadence of her heart.

She watched through the window as boys from the JV team climbed out the back of Jake's truck. A thought occurred. She hurried to open the pane. "Recycle what you can!"

"One step ahead of you." Jake grinned and pointed out three boxes marked *Plastic*, *Paper*, and *Glass*.

Kaylyn nodded and returned to her dishes and baking but couldn't resist an occasional peek outside. Each time, the boys were busy, while Jake seemed preoccupied behind his truck.

What is *he doing?*

She iced the last batch of pastries then carried the food and beverages into the dining room. A glance out the patio doors revealed her back yard also free of debris. Gratitude filled her heart as she swung open the front door. "Refreshments are ready!"

Whoops and hollers accompanied the thunder of feet as the boys made a consolidated rush toward the house.

"Wash up. Food's in the dining room."

Kaylyn watched Jake close the tailgate and emerge from behind his truck carrying a box.

He held it toward her, a twinkle in his eyes.

Kaylyn slanted him a half-suspicious gaze. "What's this?"

"See for yourself."

She opened the container and pulled out an antique metal pitcher filled with slightly limp flowers. A mixture of yellow, orange, and pink blooms from her wind-hammered Lantana shrubs dotted a heart-shaped wreath made of twigs. A somewhat battered bow tied together a dozen surprisingly unscathed roses.

"Thank you, Jake!" She brushed her lips across his cheek, but a quick move on his part turned the gesture into a surprise kiss.

Barely there. Just enough. *A promise of more.*

Kaylyn stepped away and met his warm gaze with a shaky smile. "Recycling at its very best."

The End

Dear Reader,

Like Kaylyn, how often do we let life get in the way of love and romance? We may love our families, friends, even ourselves. I believe when God said, "let us make man in our image," it was because life is meant to be shared. True, after the passing of your heart/soul mate, loving another will never be the same. Do it anyway! Find yourself. Find a new companion. Create a new normal. Live. Love. Be happy. And share that joy with others. We are not meant to be alone.

Remember, love isn't love until you give it away.

Something to think about.

"Inspirational with an Edge!" ™

Old Flame ~ New Love

"Good morning Mrs. West." Lindsay moved her shopping cart out of the way so the lady could pass. Instead, she stopped alongside hers, blocking the aisle. Thankfully there weren't many people in the store this morning.

'Morning, Lindsay. Where are you planning to spend Thanksgiving?"

Lindsay shrugged. "Not sure, yet. I usually go to the cabin."

The place that had saved her life years before still remained a haven of peace and quiet when Lindsay needed respite from her normal routine. "Will you be cooking or visiting this year?"

Mrs. West's toothless grin made her heart sing.

"Hosting. Everyone is bringing food to my house."

"That's wonderful."

"Yes, it is! The whole gang will be there, even Stephen and his girls."

Lindsay's heart tremored at the mention of the younger of the two West boys. "Oh? Is he still married?"

How rude! She admonished herself mentally.

Mrs. West's sigh had Lindsay's eyebrow quirking in question. "No. Knew that wasn't going to last, no matter how hard he tried. Bless his heart. She just wasn't right for him. Y'know?"

When Lindsay refrained from comment, she continued. "Anyway, he's moved back and into an apartment for now. Once they get the messy details out of the way, I'm sure he'll be looking for another home."

A gleam lit her ancient eyes. "I'll have to tell him to hire you to decorate."

Lindsay ignored the shiver that shook her heart at the thought of her high school crush, single again and back in town. She maneuvered the cart out of another shopper's way. "You do that."

"Well, dear, if you don't go off to that little place in the mountains, you're welcome to have lunch with us."

"I'll remember that. Thank you."

Lindsay arrived home and had barely put her groceries away when the phone rang. Caller ID showed Mrs. West's daughter on the line. She answered with a smile. "Hey, Gayle."

"Hey, Linds. Mom said she ran into you at the grocery store and invited you to celebrate Thanksgiving with us. We'd love to have you."

"Thanks, Gayle. I appreciate the invite and will keep it in mind."

Lindsay replaced the receiver with a sigh. No one, not even his sister–one of her closest friends–knew of her feelings for Stephen. Feelings that hadn't dimmed over the years despite her two marriages–one which ended in divorce, the other in widowhood.

Shaking off the dark mood threatening to overtake her, Lindsay went out to her workshop and poured over the designs for her next decorating project. She began creating some of the décor she would use to fulfill her client's requests only to be interrupted a half dozen times, or more, for flower arrangements and centerpieces for the upcoming holiday festivities.

On Thanksgiving eve, Lindsay sat on the edge of her bed. Forecasts of freezing rain, sleet, ice, and snow had put the quietus on any thought she had of travelling to her cabin. Gayle and Mrs. West's invitation rang in her ears. She picked up her husband's picture, pressing it against her heart. *What should I do?*

She saw his face, heard his voice, and felt his arms around her. *Live, love, be happy.* The warm glow that had always accompanied his smile filled her heart. Her decision made, she put the picture down and slid beneath the covers.

The next day dawned bright and clear. Lindsay breathed in the crisp air. Leaves crunched underfoot as she walked the two blocks to her destination. Standing on Mrs. West's porch, she juggled the huge centerpiece she'd put together and rang the bell. Stephen opened the door. His eyes widened. Pleasure lit his gaze.

"Lindsay! What a surprise! Come in, come in!"

Before she could untangle the knots in her tongue, he'd pulled her into the house, kissed both cheeks and ushered her into the kitchen where the family had gathered around the island. "Look who's here."

"How beautiful!" Mrs. West relieved Lindsay of the arrangement as each of her children moved forward in greeting.

First Gayle. "I'm so glad you decided to join us."

"Mom told us you might come." This from the elder daughter, Mary.

And Clyde, the oldest son: "Good to see you again,

Lindsay."

"I hear you have your own business," Stephen remarked, handing her a glass of wine.

Lindsay sipped and swallowed the nerves clogging her throat. "Yes, flower shop, home decorating, interior design. I also do a bit of landscaping and Feng Shui."

His eyebrows arched in interest. "Really? My apartment is bare bones."

Lindsay smiled, warmed by the interest in his eyes. "Give me a call and we'll see what we can do about that."

He touched his glass to hers. "Sounds like a plan."

The End

Dear Reader,

Lindsay's high school crush was one she never truly forgot despite the love she shared with her husband. Don't we all have someone like this in our life? An old flame. A secret crush. A special someone who makes our heart sing with hope. Our soul longs for what's possible, what 'might have been.' It's never wrong to remember this/these person/people with fondness.

What's unhealthy is getting so wrapped up in the 'what ifs' of your fantasy life that you ignore the blessings in your reality. We tend to think romance alone brings on that flood of chemicals 'hich make our soul sing. In reality, we can generate that feeling simply by thinking about and thanking God for the blessings in our life.

Basking in the good will generate those same

thrilling emotions flowing through your body, filling your heart, and crowding your mind. Try it sometimes! It may take practice but eventually you'll feel the depths of love God, the creator of the universe, pours out upon you.

If you don't know Him already, I pray you'll seek Him with your whole heart, mind, soul and body and that you'll be blessed beyond measure as a result.

Love Field

Katie Clarkson grabbed her carryon bag from the overhead bin and made her way up the aisle to disembark from the plane. Murmurs of 'Merry Christmas' and 'Happy Holidays,' warmed her spirit despite the ache in her heart that she'd spend Christmas alone.

Again.

She resisted the urge to rub the spot in her chest that hurt every time she thought about her parents, who'd died within hours of each other. She hadn't been back to the small Louisiana town since she'd settled, and sold, their estate nearly five years ago.

Katie's grief eased, quickly replaced by a sense of hope, and a hint of joy as lights blinked in tandem with cheery tunes of snowmen and reindeer. Mixed with more poignant songs of the season, they reminded her to reflect on the blessings in her life.

Grabbing the first available tram, Katie headed to the gate where she'd await her connecting flight. Stopping at a café, she ordered a sandwich and fruit, picked up bottles of tea and water then continued to the lounging area. She settled in a chair next to one of the tables and prepared to savor her midnight snack. The advantage of low airfare outweighed the late flights and long layovers. Katie enjoyed the time spent in relative solitude watching people, listening to music, or reading.

Summer gave way to fall in the span of a weekend and cold weather had rushed in, ending her previous stint yesterday. Her next position started within a few days, so downtime in an airport was not an imposition, but a luxury.

Her job as a National Parks Ranger kept her in the hub of things. Always busy. Sometimes hectic. Forever exciting. She loved moving from one place to another. One day, though, she'd find her soul mate and they'd travel together until the time came to settle and raise a family. Or perhaps they'd continue to move around and work while homeschooling the children. Both options had their own special appeal. Katie was perfectly content to see which hand of cards life dealt, and to take every day, each park and adventure, as it came.

A shuffle and thud snagged her attention. Katie turned and watched as a tall, lanky man strolled into the lobby. Their eyes met. He smiled. Her pulse stuttered then scrambled. She forced down the bite of bread, meat and cheese lodged in her throat with a gulp of tea.

"Late night traveler too, I see." The velvety-rough tone of his voice sent delicious shivers along her nerve endings.

Katie nodded, too tongue-tied to speak.

"Ranger or Jr. Ranger?"

Katie shifted in her chair, adjusted her cap. "Ranger. You?" She indicated his attire with a wave.

He laughed and offered his hand. "Judson Stiles, National Parks Ranger at your service, Ma'am."

Her cheeks warmed but Katie shook the proffered hand. A shiver traversed her spine at the sense of recognition his grasp sparked. Maybe she wouldn't be alone for the holidays after all.

"You barely look old enough to be a Jr. Ranger."

Katie resisted rolling her eyes at the familiar statement. At twenty-five, being told she looked twelve was more often an irritation than compliment. "I became a Jr. Ranger at the age of five. Every summer my parents and I visited different states, various parks. By the time I was a teenager I knew I wanted to work in the National Parks system. I've been to, or worked at, nearly all in the lower forty-eight, Alaska and Hawaii."

"Sounds like my life. Where are you headed now?"

Katie swallowed the hard knot of emotion that rose to choke her from talking about her parents. "California."

"Ah, someplace warm for the winter and snowmen made of sand."

She let out a self-conscious little laugh. "Yeah, I'm definitely a summer person. Spring and fall are fine but, come winter I want to be as warm as I can get."

"Me too. Chin up girl. New Year in a new location equals new opportunities."

"Yeah, but first we've got to get through Christmas." Something in her demeanor must have hinted at her pain because he reached over and touched her hand. Awareness and a sense of knowing sizzled between them. Katie fought the urge to curl up in his arms and bawl her eyes out, smiled instead, and removed her hand from beneath his.

They sat in silence for a few minutes. She finished her sandwich, offered him the fruit. He declined.

The hours flew by with long stretches of

conversation interspersed with companionable silence. Katie couldn't believe how much she and Judson had in common — from their love of wildlife and nature and similar childhoods, to mirroring dreams and goals for the future.

At a break in conversation, he rose. "Going to grab a coffee. Would you mind watching my bag?"

"Not at all. Although that is against airport security." Her grin took the sting out of the words. Excitement trembled in her core at his husky little laugh.

"I promise there is nothing in there airport security would need to worry over."

Ten minutes later he returned and handed her a cup marked Caramel Latte.

"And how did you know this is my favorite coffee?"

He shrugged. "Lucky guess I'm sure."

But Katie knew better. It went without saying her soul mate would know her likes, dislikes and innermost desires. After all, she'd hoped and prayed, dreamed of and planned for him since she was a little girl. "Funny how we've traveled virtually the same path all of our lives and haven't met before now."

Laughter rumbled from somewhere deep in Judson's broad chest. He winked. "Guess this airport isn't called Love Field for nothing."

The End

Dear Reader,

I remember a song from the 80's by Savage Garden where the singer croons that he knew his love before they met and that he'd dreamed them into life.

Have you ever thought this about someone or some instance? Like you've met someone or been somewhere before? Some call this intuition. Others, déjà vu. And yet others, divine intervention. Whatever, we've all experienced it at some point in our lives.

I wonder how much wiser and more receptive we'd be if we paid attention and acknowledged those little moments as messages from God?

Something to think about!

If you don't know HIM already, I pray you will seek a personal relationship with the Lord, Jesus Christ and if you do, that you'll continue to draw closer to Him and in all things you will give Him praise!

About the Author

Pamela S. Thibodeaux grew up in the town of Iowa, Louisiana. She is the mother of four (two by blood and two by marriage) and a grandmother. A deeply committed Christian, Pamela firmly believes in God and His promises.

"God is very real to me, and I feel people today need and want to hear more of His truths wherever they can glean them. People are hungry for practical (and real) Christian values, not some 'holier-than-thou' dictates which are impossible to believe and difficult to live up to," Pamela says.

"I do my best to encourage readers to develop a personal relationship with God. The deepest desire of my heart is to glorify God and to get His message of faith, trust, and forgiveness to a hurting world."

Email Pamela at: pam@pamelathibodeaux.com
Visit her website:
http://www.pamelathibodeaux.com

Sign up to receive **Pam's Newsletter** and get a FREE short story.

Also: be sure to follow Pam on Social Media: FaceBook, Twitter @psthib, Instagram, GoodReads, and BookBub.

Other Titles by Pamela S. Thibodeaux

A Hint of Romance ~ Collection of Short Stories
Whether married or looking for another chance at romance, love is always in the air for these couples…

Twin Flames: Will twins Ray and Raelee MacFarland get a second chance at love after her husband runs off with his wife?

Like a Rock: Will Macey and Jerry's love survive midlife crisis and empty nest syndrome?

The Big Catch: Will Karla come to love fishing as much as Jeff or will his passion for a rod and reel tangle up their relationship?

A Hero for Jessica: Will a "champion" lawyer and the author of romantic suspense find love written in their future?

In His Sight: Can the relationship between a teacher with the gift of prophecy and a single mother on the run from her deranged ex-husband withstand the tragedy lurking on the horizon?

Review of Love: Can two people who clash over what each perceives as *professional writing* suspend their judgmental attitudes and find true love?

Paper Roses: Will a homecoming tradition give Patti Howard a chance at love with her son's football coach?

Journey's End: Will Ellie's dream of seeing the world come true with a new man or will she be resigned to staying put and living vicariously through her granddaughter?

Soul Mates: Will Jolie and her soul mate reconnect once again, or will she live another lifetime without him?

Tempered Hearts (book 1 in Tempered series)

An innocent veterinarian. A jaded cowboy. Will they get burned under a Texas sun or find the heat that leads to happily ever after?

Craig Harris has sworn off relationships. He's been burned and betrayed too many times to count. But when he crosses paths with the hot-tempered veterinarian his grandfather hired for the summer will he let go of hurt and mistrust to find the true love he's always longed for?

Tamera Collins is in no mood to put up with an arrogant jerk cowboy even if he is her boss. Grieving too-recent losses leaves her wary of the strong attraction between her and Craig. Can she overcome heartache and shattered faith and open up to their blossoming love?

Tempered Dreams (book 2 in Tempered Series)

He took an oath to preserve life. Can he stick to it when the woman he loves is in jeopardy?

Dr. Scott Hensley (introduced in Tempered Hearts) has built a wall around his heart since the death of his wife and parents. Katrina Simmons is recovering from scars inflicted on her as a battered wife. Can dreams be renewed and faith strengthened? Can they find joy and peace in God's love and in love for one another?

Tempered Fire (book 3 in Tempered Series)

The daughter of a wealthy rancher… A nobody from nowhere with nothing… Will their love survive?

Amber Harris is a good girl on the brink of womanhood. Stanley Morrison is a young man at the start of his life. For each other, they have always felt the fireworks that two people in love should feel. But the questions about his past, his pride, and Amber's father might be the end of what could be a strong relationship. As the two try to protect their budding romance, some unlikely but powerful forces conspire to keep them apart. Will they survive the wishes of everyone around them with their relationship intact?

Tempered Joy (book 4 in Tempered series)

He's an 'all around' cowboy. She thinks rodeo cowboys have rocks for brains and a death wish for a soul.

All around rodeo cowboy and heir to the Rockin' H Ranch, Ace Harris is determined not to fall in love. He's only loved one woman in his life, his mother, and no one can even come close to filling her boots. Lexie Morgan thinks rodeo cowboys have rocks for brains and a death wish for a soul. A broken childhood and the death of her father and best friend leave her doubting and questioning God (despite her years of religious upbringing) and afraid of love. Can two young people who clash from the onset learn to trust in the healing power of God and find love and happiness amidst tragedy and grief?

Tempered Truth (book 5 in the Tempered Series)

Will the truth set them free, or will it destroy a lifelong friendship?

Fate declared them neighbors. Scandal insisted they were brothers. The fact that they looked enough alike to be twins only added fuel to the rumors flying about their parentage.

For fifty-plus years Craig Harris and Scott Hensley have enjoyed a bond nothing can sever.

Not the insinuations that they share the same father.

Not the years of strife and grief and heartache.

Not even death.

Will the truth set them free, or will it destroy the friendship that has lasted a lifetime?

Tempered Journey (book 6 in Tempered series)

She's second-guessing her life choices. He's been widowed for over a decade. Will a case of mistaken identity bring two lonely souls together?

As a Registered Nurse and Energy Medicine Practitioner, Pat Greene has spent her entire life in service to others. But when her BFF finds true love for the second time, she finds herself surprisingly envious. Has her call to service—which she will never regret—somehow caused her to miss out on something special? The loneliness she's kept at bay gnaws at her heart. While in Bandera, Texas she has a chance encounter with the one man she's ever truly loved and is shocked to then discover he's ***not*** the man she thought he was.

The ache of loss still haunts Craig Harris a decade after his wife's death. Has his loyalty to her memory closed off his heart? Is he bound to an existence without the soul-deep joy he knows a woman's love can bring? Then he meets Pat Greene. Unprepared, he is bowled over by an instant, powerful spark of attraction—the kind he hasn't allowed himself to feel for years.

There's no mistaking the allure the handsome

cowboy holds for Pat, but the idea of giving up a lifetime of missionary work sets off a firestorm of doubt and indecision. Besides, Craig has children, grandchildren, and extended family members to think about.

The fact she mistakes him for his brother, with whom she had a brief relationship decades ago, tempers the initial magnetism that draws Craig toward Pat, but the more they get to know one another, the more he wants her in his life.

Will love be enough to tame the wanderlust in her soul and open his heart to the possibilities a future together might hold?

Tempered Journey is a later-in-life romance that shows the power of love to heal the loneliest of hearts. This novel brings together characters from the *Tempered* series and *My Heart Weeps*. We catch up with Melena and Garrett as well as Mike, Trina, and the rest of the Harris/Hensley clan as we journey into love with Craig Harris and Pat Greene. Get your copy today and fall in love with these characters all over again.

Lori's Redemption

Can a notorious bad girl find redemption & win the cowboy preacher's heart?

Lori Strickland (introduced in *Tempered Fire*) has always been known as her father's "wild child" with no desire to change until she meets ex-bull-rider-turned-preacher, Rafe Judson. Her attempts to change her wanton ways come to naught until she realizes redemption only comes with true repentance. Can she find redemption and win the heart of the cowboy preacher?

My Heart Weeps

When life takes everything, your world stops. Can a retreat heal the broken lives of two wounded souls?

Melena Rhyker's world shattered the day her husband died. Lost without the man of her dreams, she digs deep to find a path out of her sorrow. Discovering an artistic retreat, she vows to find a reason to carry on and focus her life in a new direction. Can she heal her own heart, and find her new beginning?

Garrett Saunders knows pain. He's spent most of his life hiding from his past. Regrets and lies haunt him, but he longs to leave them behind and embrace his true self. Will Melena's efforts to rebuild her life in the face of such grief encourage him to exorcise his own demons of guilt and shame?

Will two hurting people find peace, wholeness and perhaps love in the heart of Texas?

Get this second chance women's fiction novel today and see how love and faith conquers all.

Kyleigh's Cowboy

She's attempting to start a new life. He's roamed for more than a decade. Can they let go of the past and grab hold of the future?

Seven years after the death of her husband, Kyleigh Winters turned their old vacation home into a brand new guest ranch. Not willing to join the ranks of lonely women trolling the bars or online in search of a man, Kyleigh is sure if God wishes her to have another husband, He'll send the perfect someone in His own time. But will she be open to the possibility of new love when He does?

Searching for a place that calls to his soul, Lance Stevens has been a roaming cowboy for ten years since retiring from the Marines. He finds that sanctuary the moment he drives through the Silver Star's gate and meeting the lovely owner speaks to more than his soul. Will he open to the healing power of love?

Get Pamela Thibodeaux's second chance romance novella today and see how love and faith conquers all.

Keri's Christmas Wish

Controversy and Inconsistencies are thieves of holiday joy for Keri... Is there any hope for a happy holiday season?

For as long as she can remember, Keri Jackson has despised the hype and commercialism around Christmas—especially with the controversy over the time of Jesus' birth. Will she get her wish and be free of the angst to truly enjoy Christmas this year?

Jeremy Hinton thinks Keri is a highly intelligent, deeply emotional, and intensely complex woman and he's as fascinated by her aversion to Christmas as he is of the woman herself. A devout Christian at heart, he's studied all of the world's religions and homeopathic healing modalities. But when a rare bacterial infection threatens her life, will all of his faith and training be for naught?

Fans of near death experiences will enjoy this woman's mystical journey into spiritual Truth.

Circles of Fate

When two souls are torn apart by duty, can the

hand of God bring them back to a happily ever after?

Late Vietnam War era. Strapped for cash, Todd Jameson flirts with disaster. Caught robbing a liquor store to pay for his dad's funeral and given the choice of jail or signing up for the military, he picks the best of two bad options and joins the army. But just as his fresh start reconnects him with a sense of honor and the friendship of a gracious woman, he's deployed overseas into an unknown destiny.

Sixteen-year-old Shaunna Chatman devotes every breath to caring for her sick mother. Working in a diner to make ends meet, the last thing on her agenda is to fall for a young soldier about to be sent into battle. But when he encourages her not to wait, she reluctantly moves on to wed another who's there to pick up the pieces after she buries her beloved mom.

Thrown into a whirlwind of circumstance, Todd flows in and out of the courageous girl's narrative wondering if their stories will ever fully entwine. And though Shaunna's journey grants her a child even as personal tragedy strikes, her thoughts often turn to the boy who still fills her heart.

Will their paths merge once more to bask in the glory of His love?

Circles of Fate is a deeply woven inspirational women's fiction novel. If you like believable heroes, roads to enlightenment, and tales of inner strength, then you'll adore Pamela S Thibodeaux's romantic saga.

The Visionary

Will the ugly secret haunting the twins keep them

from finding true love?

While most visionaries see into the future, Taylor sees the past. but only as it pertains to her work. Hailed by her peers as "a visionary with an instinct for beauty and an eye for the unique" Taylor is undoubtedly a brilliant architect and gifted designer. But she and twin brother Trevor share more than a successful business. The two share a childhood wrought with lies and deceit and the kind of abuse that's disturbingly prevalent in today's society.

Can the love of God and the awesome healing power of His grace and mercy free the twins from their past and open their hearts to the good plan and the future He has for their lives?

Love is a Rose (devotional)

Can God use a secular song to speak to someone and touch their heart?

Music is the magical entry into the spirit world, the golden gate into the Kingdom of God. But we mustn't be of the mindset that God only uses Christian music to reach out and touch our mind, heart, and spirit. God uses any and **every** means available to speak to His children.

Our job is to be open and receptive.

In this devotional, Pamela S Thibodeaux shares how God opened her spirit to a deeper understanding of the abundance of His grace and mercy through the words of the song, The Rose sung by Country & Western artist Conway Twitty.

Pamela offers Seeds to Ponder and a prayer as she parallels the love of God and the Christian life to each verse of the song.

***Love's Overcoming Power* eBook**

Temptation, Abuse, Grief, and Doubt are plagues common to women all over the world. In John, 16 Jesus said.... In the world you will have tribulation but be of good cheer, for I have overcome the world.

In this Women's Fiction collection comprised of three full-length novels and one novella, Pamela S Thibodeaux shares stories that exemplify the power of God's love to overcome whatever situations life throws at you.

Includes: ***The Visionary, Circles of Fate, My Heart Weeps*** and ***Keri's Christmas Wish.***

***The Tempered Series Collection* eBook**

Start at the beginning and follow these beloved characters throughout the years as love crosses the lines of age and strengthens the bonds of friendship.

Contains: ***Tempered Hearts, Tempered Dreams, Tempered Fire, Tempered Joy, Lori's Redemption***

Praise for Pamela S. Thibodeaux

*"**Kyleigh's Cowboy** was so beautifully written, that it literally made me cry. The hero and heroine were sympathetic yet flawed and I fell instantly in love with them. Wonderful Christian Cowboy Romance!" ~ Amazon Reviewer T.P. Warren*

*"Pamela Thibodeaux uses her masterful story writing art to create a powerful story of how God heals a woman's heart —broken by grief— through recovery, love and triumph." ~ CBA Best-Selling Author DiAnn Mills on **My Heart Weeps**.*

*"Loved this book. Wish everyone could read this. Definitely puts all holidays in perspective. If we remember the reason for the holidays then we must put God first... Always. I will certainly recommend this book. Great stuff keep up the great writing." ~ (Amazon) Review of **Keri's Christmas Wish** by Reba*

*"Oh, the passion, faith and just LIFE that flows through this book... Powerful writing indeed!" ~ Review of **Circles of Fate** by Deena Peterson, Book Reviewer @ A Peek at my Bookshelf and Just One More*

*"Thibodeaux leads the reader through from the first page to the last without once relinquishing control. She hooks them, holds them, and keeps them enthralled until the last line." ~ Review of **The Visionary** by Delia Latham, author of the "Solomon's Gate" series*

"If you have ever considered Christian fiction bland, then check out the **Tempered Series.** *It will be well worth your time."* ~ Amanda Killgore for Huntress Reviews

"Lori's Redemption *is fast paced, lots of action, gripping storyline... I loved it. It's gone straight back into my TBR pile."* ~ Clare Revell author of the *"Monday's Child"* series

"Through Pamela's blessed ability to find God everywhere, even in secular song lyrics, she has written devotions guaranteed to touch the heart and remind the reader of our True Love, the Rose of Sharon." ~ *Endorsement for* **Love is a Rose** *by Linda Yezak, Author, Editor Triple Edge Critique Service*

Once again.....Thank You...

I pray you are as blessed as I am by your purchase of this book. If you enjoy *A Hint of Holiday Romance,* please write a positive review, and post it at online retailers and websites where readers gather and/or your social media platforms (FaceBook, Good Reads, BookBub, Twitter, etc).

If you haven't already, sign up to receive my *Newsletter* and get a FREE short story.

*Temperance
Publishing*